Sen Loi

R. Annan

Printed in the United States of America

Published by One Vision Publishing

E-BOOK ISBN: 978-1-942338-19-2

PRINT BOOK ISBN: 978-1-942338-18-5

WGA Reg. # R30042 (O2/11/2013)

Dedicated to

Jasmine

Tony

Laura

And

My Beloved Angel, Elke

1.

On a balmy, sunny day in April, a black four-door sedan drove past palm trees and green lawns in northeast Kowloon. It came to a large gated estate, stopped momentarily at the guard post, then continued up a long gravel road to an oval courtyard. It went around the courtyard and stopped in front of a large oriental house with an ornate front door.

Young Police Inspector John Marion, immaculately dressed in tropical whites with matching hat and shoes, got out of the passenger's side and went around to speak to Detective Somes, the driver. Somes looked more like a boxer than a policeman.

"You wait here, Somes," Marion said. "This shouldn't take long."

"You best be careful sir," Somes cautioned, "they say she's pretty shifty."

"So I've heard," Marion said. He turned and walked up to the front door and rapped loudly on it.

A young oriental face appeared in a small window in the upper section of the door. It stared at the Inspector for a moment and then a hand came up and opened the window sideways.

Marion pulled a small white card from his pocket and handed it through the window. The hand took the card and closed the window. Moments later the door opened and Marion entered.

The inside of the house almost took the Englishman's breath away. It was pure vintage Chinese. There was a foyer, a great room, and a chess room. A teakwood staircase led up to the second floor. In the rear of the great room was a door to a kitchen from which emanated the scents of garlic, onion, and basil. He stood alone inhaling the delicious aroma for a moment, and then walked through the foyer into the great room. He stood there looking around until he saw the small chess room to his right. He stared at it for a moment, and then went in.

Marion noticed the chess table where a board revealed a chess game was in progress. One set of figures was white marble and the other set was green jade. He picked up a jade pawn, looked at it for a second, and then tossed it high into the air, catching it as it came down.

"Careful, Inspector," a soft voice behind him said. For a moment he was startled and almost dropped the chess piece. "It's very old and valuable," the feminine voice said.

He had heard about her. They said she was wicked and beautiful and dangerous. Her lips dripped poison and she carried a hidden knife, they said. She could sneak up on you and cut your throat so quick you wouldn't even know it until you were about to die. She had sold her soul to the devil and would live forever. Don't turn your back on her, they said. The only one who could ever get close to her, the story went, was old Chief Inspector Barnes. Yes, she wouldn't try anything with old Barnes. Maybe she had Barnes under her thumb, like dozens of others. Or was it the other way around? Who knew?

No one would ever know now. It was too late for that.

Marion carelessly tossed the pawn on the chess table and turned around. For a moment he was stunned, but quickly recovered.

"Chief Inspector Barnes said you were a stunner. He was quite right," Marion said, removing his hat. The two of them were boldly staring eye to eye.

This woman was more beautiful than they had said. She was as tall as he was in her sandals, and had jet-black hair that covered her shoulders. Her body was slim and tapered with flaring hips. The v of her qipao revealed much. One leg showed, from the knee down, through the slit in her dress. But it was that sensuous face, the deep, black, penetrating, almond-shaped eyes and full lips that held Marion helpless for a moment.

"He called me a stunner, did he?" Sen Loi asked in a voice smooth as silk. "Shame on the old charmer!" She smiled seductively.

Sen Loi went around Marion, almost brushing up against him. He inhaled her perfume. She picked up the jade pawn and set it back in its place, then completed her walk around to face him.

"I suppose the Chief Inspector sent you to tease me, did he not?" she said. "How sweet of him. But you can tell him I am still angry at him for not coming last night to finish our little chess game."

Marion's face turned serious. "I'm afraid the Chief Inspector won't be playing chess with you from now on, madam."

"Oh? And why is that? Doesn't the old charmer love Sen Loi anymore?"

"He is dead, madam," the Inspector said gravely, closely watching Sen Loi's face for a reaction.

"Oh?"

Sen Loi turned her back and walked slowly into the great room. She stood at the large teak table with her back to Marion. He waited a moment then followed her.

"Did you hear what I said, madam? I said…"

"I hear quite well, Inspector, thank you!"

"Well, as the Chief Inspector's friend, you…"

Sen Loi turned to face Marion. "And who do you suspect of murdering the Chief Inspector?"

"Murder? I never said that he was murdered, did I?"

"No, but he was, was he not?"

"Oh, indeed he was madam! His throat was cut from ear to ear! They almost popped his head off!"

Marion kept staring at the woman's face, trying to read it, but it showed him nothing.

"The night before last, we played chess until very late. Then he left, saying he had to attend to something," Sen Loi said. "Ah, just where was he found, Inspector?"

"Behind your gambling hall, the Blue Dragon."

"I see."

Suddenly a tiny, old, shriveled-up, hunched over Chinese woman came into the great room carrying a tray of tea and cookies. She set it on the table and looked over at the Inspector.

"Another *gueillo*, huh?" she said in Chinese. "Bah!" She retreated slowly back into the kitchen.

Marion chuckled. "So, I'm a white ghost, am I?"

"That was my cook, Kha," Sen Loi said. "She doesn't like strangers, I'm afraid. Will you take tea, Inspector?"

"Tea? No, this isn't a social call, madam," Marion said. "It's strictly official."

"Oh, that sounds so serious, Inspector. Are you going to arrest me?"

"Isn't that why the Chief Inspector came here last night, to arrest you, madam? Is that why you had him killed?"

"If I had him killed, do you think I would hide his body behind the Blue Dragon? Does that make any sense to you, Inspector?"

"It could be a clever ploy to make you look innocent, I'd say."

"Assuming I did have the Chief Inspector murdered, what would be my motive?"

"Your motive? Perhaps Barnes was on to your opium operations and…"

"Please go on, Inspector."

"…and your white slavery business, as well," Marion said, summing up his theory.

Sen Loi smiled, "Opium, no, white slavery, no. But you forgot that I do run guns. Are you going to arrest me for that, Inspector?"

Marion sneered. "What do you do with all that blood money from your dirty little enterprises, madam?"

"That which you call, 'blood money', Inspector, is put to good use."

Marion chuckled. "Oh, really? Come now, madam. Tell me, how do you spend it? New dresses? Cars? What?"

"That money is used to buy medical supplies and. guns. My country is being invaded, or haven't you heard?"

"Yes, I've heard. But, there's no war going on here. Just a crime wave and you're a big part of it."

Sen Loi laughed cynically. "No, there is no war here yet, but it will come soon enough. And when it does come, it will catch you British with you trousers down around your ankles."

The Inspector sighed. "Well I'm no politician. I'm just an officer of the law. I think Chief Inspector Barnes was just about to arrest you, so you had him murdered."

"But you have no evidence to back that up, do you? If you did, we wouldn't be standing here talking, would we, sir?"

The Inspector sniffled and looked away, then back. "Oh, I'll get the evidence, madam. In the meantime, I'll be watching your every move. Just one slip and I'll have you swinging from the gallows with a noose around that pretty neck. Rest assured of that."

They stood face to face for a moment smiling, but not in a friendly way. Sen Loi finally said, "So, is that how it stands, Inspector?"

"Yes, that's how it stands. I'm coming after you, madam. You're on notice. I'm serious. I'm not beating around the bush."

Sen Loi suddenly chuckled. "Beating around the bush? That's an activity which we Chinese have no use for, Inspector."

"What was that, madam?"

"Oh, nothing, is there something else you would like to accuse me of while you're here, Inspector?"

"If you think this is amusing, madam, it is not! This is very serious business!"

"Indeed it is, Inspector. Indeed it is."

"The next time you see me, madam, I may be coming to arrest you. Think about that and let it be your guide."

The Inspector looked around, "Good. Good-bye, then."

2.

Sen Loi sighed and waited until she heard the car drive away. She got the tea tray and took it into the kitchen and put it on the table. Kha was working over the stove. Sen Loi called out and the Chinese girl, the same one that answered the door, came in from the garden with a sprig of rosemary. She handed it to Kha.

"So, they finally got the old Chief Inspector, did they? The rats!" Kha said.

"Yes, and now the British are out to make my life miserable and I can't be bothered with them right now. I have important things to do."

The girl, Sue Lin, asked, "Who would want to kill that nice old man anyway? He was so sweet."

"Yes…why? That is the question, isn't it?"

"There are so many evil people here in Kowloon. And spies are everywhere. The French, the German, the Japanese, and the Americans. So many of them," Sue Lin lamented.

Kha cleared her throat for attention. "I had a dream last night. A rabbit went crazy and killed a wolf." She paused for effect, but no one said anything. So she went on. "That means big trouble for this house."

Sen Loi laughed. "You and your dreams, old one."

"That Inspector means trouble," Kha insisted.

Sue Lin spoke up enthusiastically. "I could seduce him for you, Mistress, if you want me to. I could boggle his mind just like that!" Sue Lin snapped her fingers.

Suddenly they heard a car pull up and the front door opened. Kha became alert. "Shush! The *gueillo* is returning!"

"No," Sen Loi said. "It is only Pug, grandmother."

The front door closed and there were footsteps in the great room. Pug, Sen Loi's chauffeur, came into the kitchen, his cap in his hand, ducking down so as not to bump his bald bullet-shaped head. He was an oriental giant dressed in a dark blue chauffeur's uniform with leg guards and shoes. He had a flat, scarred face that had taken many blows. The kitchen chair squeaked as he sat down on it.

"Any trouble, Pug?" Sen Loi asked.

"No, mistress. Everything went as planned. The shipment of food and guns are on the way over the Kowloon border."

"Have you heard about the Chief Inspector, little bear?" Kha asked.

"Yes," Pug said. "It is all over Kowloon. Very sad."

"The police were just here," Sen Loi said. "It seems that I'm their prime suspect."

Pug nodded. "That's not good. It's going to interfere with business."

"Yes," Sen Loi said. "Come with me, Pug."

Pug followed Sen Loi into the great room where she sat down at a desk next to a bookshelf, near the kitchen door. She opened a drawer and took out a large envelope. She took a packet of money from it and handed that to Pug.

"See what our informants can learn about the Chief Inspector's killers," Sen Loi said. "No one in Kowloon does anything without someone else knowing what was done and who did it."

Pug chuckled and secured the money in the breast pocket of his uniform. "That's for sure. A chicken can fart in

Tsuen Wan and they will smell it in Tai Po! And if we find out who did the dirty deed?"

"The Chief Inspector was a very dear friend. Let that speak for itself."

Suddenly Kha yelled from the kitchen, "Come, little bear, you must be hungry."

"Indeed I am, grandmother," Pug roared out. "I'm so hungry I could eat a dead horse!" He quickly headed for the kitchen, just as Sue Lin came out. She stood beside the desk.

"Mistress," Sue Lin said. "Do you think Pug has a girlfriend in town?"

Sen Loi chuckled. "I don't think so. No, I'm pretty sure he doesn't."

"How can you be so sure?"

"Because Pug is a eunuch," Sen Loi replied.

"A what?"

"A eunuch. You know what a eunuch is, don't you?"

"Hmmmm…oh, that!"

"Yes, that."

"How do you know?"

"It's none of your business how I know," Sen Loi insisted.

"So…how did it happen?"

"I don't know. He never talks about it, but I suspect there's an interesting story there."

"Gee…maybe I should ask him."

"What makes you think he'll tell you?"

"Well, we're like brother and sister. He really likes me," Sue Lin said.

"Then, by all means, ask him," Sen Loi said.

"You mean right now?"

"If not now, when? Go! But just get out of my hair. I have work to do."

Sue Lin went slowly off into the kitchen. Sen Loi sat, listening and waiting.

She heard Kha say, "And what do you want, little flea? Are you so hungry you could eat a dead horse, too?"

"Noooooo!" Sue Lin said. "I just want to talk to dear, sweet Pug, that's all."

"Don't bother me, little one. Can't you see I am eating?" Pug said, with a mouthful of food.

"I was just curious about…"

"About what?" Pug said very abruptly. He didn't sound like he was in a good mood.

Sue Lin sighed and said, "Well, about, uh, about, oh, never mind. It's not very important."

Sen Loi, who heard every word, burst out laughing. Suddenly Sue Lin came running out of the kitchen and confronted her.

"It wasn't that funny, Mistress," Sue Lin whined.

"That depends which side of the door you were on," Sen Loi chuckled.

Sue Lin ran up the staircase to her room, repeating, "It wasn't that funny, mistress."

3.

A few days later, at around mid-afternoon yellow shafts of sunlight lit up the great room. Sen Loi sat at her desk doing paperwork while Sue Lin sat at the dining room table reading the Kowloon Gazette. Finally she looked over at her mistress.

"What time is she coming? I forgot."

"She should be here any moment," Sen Loi said without looking up.

"Her picture is in today's newspaper," Sue Lin continued. "They call her, 'The Debutante of Kowloon. There's a whole article on her."

"Oh, really?"

"Yes. She and her uncle Jocko Wainwright were seen at the Sha-Tin Racetrack," Sue Lin said. "Why is she not with her parents?"

"Because they died mysteriously a few years ago, and right after that the girl suffered greatly and had a nervous collapse," Sen Loi said.

"How sad. What did her father do for a living, mistress?"

"He managed a bank over on Hong Kong Island. He owned most of it, actually."

"She must have a lot of money."

"She will, when she comes of age next year. Right now, her uncle is her legal guardian and handles her finances. She's engaged to a young officer in the Coast Guard."

Sue Lin referred to the newspaper again. "It says here that she likes animals and is a member of Lady St. John's organization to save injured race horses."

"Yes. That's why she's coming here. To solicit a donation."

Sen Loi turned in her chair to face her ward. "You know, Sue Lin, you sound like you worship this Wainwright girl. You read everything about her. And you have never even met her."

"Well, I've never met Mae West either, mistress, but I…"

Sue Lin stopped talking and listened intently. "Someone just pulled up. It could be her!"

Sen Loi heard it, too. A car drove up to the door and stopped. The vehicle's door opened and slammed shut. There were footsteps on the gravel, in the courtyard. Sue Lin put the paper down and quickly got up.

"I'll get it, mistress!"

"No you won't. You'll go into the kitchen and help Kha with tea and cookies. Lest you faint at the sight of Miss Wainwright."

Sue Lin went reluctantly into the kitchen as Sen Loi opened the door.

In a few moments a beautiful, tall, young blonde girl dressed in high heels, a gauzy, flowered dress, sun hat, and a handbag, stood in the great room. She had the blush of innocence about her that only the young and inexperienced have. She radiated health and enthusiasm. Her face was unblemished and fresh. She stood there, wide-eyed and beaming.

"What a lovely home you have, Madam Loi," the girl said, as if hypnotized. Her voice had a cheerfulness about it, with a London, upper-crust accent. Joan Wainwright was well educated, but slightly naïve. She was also extremely beautiful. "You are Madam Loi, aren't you?"

"I am," Sen Loi said. "Please sit down, won't you?"

They sat facing each other at the huge, wooden dining table. Sen Loi stared at Joan Wainwright, but the girl avoided direct eye contact. She fidgeted nervously with her handbag. There was an awkward moment.

"Lovely weather we're having, Madam Loi," the British girl said.

"Yes, we should enjoy it while we can."

Joan thought about that for a moment, then understood. "Oh, well, yes. Before the monsoons you mean."

"Yes, before the rains come." Sen Loi said.

"Yes, of course," Joan said, smiling. She removed her white summer gloves, and put them in her handbag.

Sen Loi sensed a certain uneasiness in the girl. It was obvious that she didn't mix much with what the British called the 'locals' and probably never visited one all alone without an escort. Perhaps she didn't even like them and even felt superior to them.

"Ah, how is Lady St. John, these days, Miss Wainwright?" Sen Loi ventured.

The girl smiled and relaxed a bit. She seemed glad to get an easy question. "Please call me Joan. Lady St. John is well, that is except for the gout in her left foot." Joan Wainwright waved her hands about when she spoke. Sen Loi wondered if that was nervousness or a natural habit.

"Oh, sorry to hear that. It is a very painful affliction, I hear."

"Yes and she has tried everything," Joan said seriously. "Nothing seems to work."

"Oh, then, perhaps I can help. Kha, the cook, has an excellent herb garden here. She is very knowledgeable in such matters."

"Oh, that would be nice" the girl said. "Very nice."

There was another awkward pause. Sen Loi smiled in an effort to put the girl at ease.

"And you're fiancé, Lieutenant St. John? He is in good health, I trust?"

The girl's eyes narrowed and her face clouded over a bit. "Oh, Bobby? I suppose so, I guess." She stared down at her hands a moment.

"Oh," Sen Loi said sweetly, "is something amiss between you two? I'm sorry. I didn't mean to pry!"

"Amiss? No, no, not at all." The girl didn't sound very convincing.

"Then things are going as well as expected?"

"Yes, you could say that. Well, ah, actually, no."

"Oh, how sad. Is it another woman?" It was a test question, asked very sympathetically to see how the girl would handle an intrusion into her private matters.

The girl exploded. "Ha! I wish it was only one, but it's more, much more. He's been, well, very active in the field all of a sudden, if you know what I mean?"

Sen Loi nodded in sympathy. "I understand. Young men like your Lieutenant are full of energy. Some men don't quite know how to handle it. They are easily overcome with certain overwhelming urges. The Americans have a quaint saying. They call it, 'sowing wild oats.' But I'm sure he will settle down soon, once he is married."

The girl seemed relieved by Sen Loi's words. "Do you think so?" she asked softly.

"Oh, of course! I'm certain he will soon come to his senses and realize what a treasure he has in you, Joan."

"Lady St. John makes light of it. To her, Bobby is just perfect. He can do no wrong."

"It will all resolve itself, Joan. You must believe that. Smile! Be happy!"

At that moment Sue Lin came from the kitchen with a tray of tea and cookies. She set it on the table and stood there as if hypnotized, staring at the English girl.

"Joan," Sen Loi said, "this is Sue Lin, my ward and companion."

The British girl smiled at Sue Lin. "How do you do, Sue Lin. I am happy to meet you."

Sue Lin stood speechless with her mouth open and her eyes fixed on the British girl. She didn't seem to notice her mistress was even there.

"Is Sue Lin alright?" Joan asked.

"Oh, she's fine, Joan. In fact, she is one of your most ardent admirers. She reads everything written about you in the newspapers and is a big fan of yours."

"Oh, dear," the British girl said. "You make me sound like a celebrity."

"But you are, Joan. Don't you know they call you the 'Debutante of Kowloon'?"

"Yes, I know. But I really don't like being called that. And my Uncle Jack, they call him 'Jocko.' He hates that, too. It infuriates him."

"I saw you two at Sha-Tin a few weeks ago. You and your uncle were with Bobby and Lady St. John." Sen Loi said to keep the conversation going.

"Oh, I'm sorry! I didn't see you there, Madam Loi. Forgive me."

"There is nothing to forgive. I was somewhat far away, and it was very crowded."

"Rather! And Uncle Jack was fuming. He'd lost quite a bit on the horses."

"Oh? That's regrettable. Ah, does he like to gamble, your uncle?"

"Yes, too much. Horses, cards, and dice. He's a compulsive gambler, I'm afraid."

The British girl looked down at her hands again. Sen Loi studied her for a moment.

"Joan, forgive me for saying this, but I sense that you are deeply troubled in your life," Sen Loi said. "Without your mother and father, I think you are beset on all sides by problems. Isn't that so?"

"Yes, I suppose that's true."

"And you feel helpless and at the mercy of life's events, do you not?"

"Yes," the girl said, almost on the verge of tears. Sen Loi reached across the table and put a comforting hand on Joan's arm.

"Joan, all of this will pass away. Soon you will be very happy…just as you were when your parents were alive," Sen Loi said softly. "Believe that and you will be just fine."

"That's very kind of you, Madam Loi to worry about me. I feel as if I've known you for a long time. As if we've met before."

"And, perhaps we have, Joan, in another life. Who can say?" Sen Loi pulled her hand back and smiled. "Now let's have tea and cookies, shall we?"

Sen Loi nodded to Sue Lin and her ward poured tea. Sue Lin was still a bit overwhelmed. She never took her eyes off the British girl and especially enjoyed watching her eat a cookie.

"So, Joan," Sen Loi said, "what is the mission of your organization?"

"Well, we try to save injured race horses. Otherwise they are shot, you know?"

"Yes, I do, and it is very sad. Where do you keep these horses?"

"Lady St. John leases some land near Sha-Tin."

"Have you ever seen my champion, Black Knight? He is stabled at Sha-Tin."

"Oh, indeed I have! I've even won some money betting on him. He is so handsome."

Sen Loi chuckled. "Indeed he is, Joan. And he well knows it, the show off. But he brings me money and fame, so I forgive him. Actually, he is the love of my life!" They all laughed.

Suddenly Joan looked serious again. "They told me not to come here, you know?"

"Oh? And why not?"

"They said you just might sell me into white slavery! Or even give me over to that cruel pirate, Chung-zi! Or, instead, you might just have me murdered!"

Sen Loi frowned and said, "Ah, out of curiosity, Joan, who said that to you?"

The girl suddenly looked embarrassed. "Ah…well."

"No, let me tell you, Joan. It was all of them. Lady St. John, Bobby, your uncle. All of them. They said, 'Joan, don't go there alone! Be careful of that terrible woman!' Isn't that so?"

"Well, yes, sort of. But they also said…"

"Go on. What did they also say?"

"You…you won't get angry, will you?"

"Oh, dear me," Sen Loi chuckled. "That bad, was it? But no, I promise you I will not be angry."

"Well, besides that white slavery thing, they said you are a gun-runner, an opium addict, and a Chinese spy."

"Oh, my! And hearing all this you still came? Why?"

"Well, I suppose, I was fascinated and curious about you," Joan said. "You're quite a legend, you know."

"And a notorious one, I'm quite sure!" Sen Loi said. "So, is that all they told you?"

"Ah, actually no. They also said you most likely were, perhaps I shouldn't repeat gossip of that sort."

"Well, what good is gossip if you can't repeat it Joan. Come tell me! It'll be fine!"

"They said that…" The girl stopped and looked down again.

"Yes? Come now, don't be bashful.

Joan looked down at her hands. "They said you were probably a…la-la!"

Sen Loi looked confused. "They said that I was la-la?"

"No, the girl said quickly. She spoke fast, "They said you were a lesbian!"

Sen Loi and Sue Lin burst out laughing. They laughed for a long time. Su Lin stomped one foot and held her side.

Finally Sen Loi asked Joan, "Have you ever met a lesbian, Joan?"

"Dear me, no!"

"Can you be certain about that?"

"No, I suppose not."

"Would it bother you if I were a lesbian, Joan?"

The girl stiffened her chin, raising it higher. "Bother me? Why should it? I mean, gee, after all, we're not related or anything. Gosh, we're not even close friends or anything. Right?"

"Exactly so," Sen Loi said with a warm smile. Then, in confidence, "Joan, do you understand the concept of yin and yang?"

"Yin and yang? Oh, sure. Why?"

"Do you know how that concept is applied to love?"

The British girl looked baffled. "Nooooo!"

"Well, let me put it as simply as I can. Men love women and women love men."

"Yes."

"But for some people, their love is more…well, inclusive. Do you know what I'm saying?"

Joan shook her head. "Not really."

"Ah, alright then, consider this Joan. Some streets are one-way streets and some streets are two-way streets. I prefer to travel the two-way streets," Sen Loi said. "Does that make things any clearer for you?"

"Not really, but maybe it will come to me later."

Sen Loi sighed and smiled. "Yes, perhaps it will."

Suddenly a light bulb went on in the British girl's head. "Wait! You're a bisexual!"

"Very good, Joan! Very astute of you!" Everyone laughed.

There was another awkward silence. Joan Wainwright smiled and stood up, looking around. It was so peaceful here that she felt she could stay forever.

"I should go now, Madam Loi," the girl said. "I hope I haven't overstayed. I'm sure I'm only in the way, as you have business to take care of."

"For you Joan, I have all the time in the world. Stay and we'll play cards or just chat. Sue Lin would just love to talk to you."

"Some other time, if I may?"

"Indeed you may, Joan. My door will always be open to you. Always. Day or night."

"Thank you and good-day, then," Joan said, and started for the door. Sue Lin ran into the kitchen.

"One moment," Sen Loi said. She went to her desk and picked up a check she had already written. She gave it to the British girl who looked at it.

"Wow! Oh, dear! That's quite a lot! Are you sure?"

"For the injured horses, Joan. For the dear, injured horses."

"I don't know what to say, except thanks!"

"It is my pleasure, Joan," Sen Loi said. "But hold a moment. Sue Lin has something for you."

Joan put the check in her handbag and waited. A moment later Sue Lin came hurrying from the kitchen. She handed the British girl a small paper bag.

"For Lady St. John's gout. It's special tea," Sue Lin said. She curtsied. Joan laughed.

"Why, thank you Sue Lin."

"Please come again, Miss Wainwright," Sue Lin said, shyly.

"I will, Sue Lin. I shall, I promise." She looked around." It's so peaceful here, and the herb garden smells wonderful." She grabbed Sue Lin's hand and shook it.

After Joan left, Sue Lin stared at her hand. "I shall never wash this hand again!"

Sen Loi went back to her desk and sat down. "And you're as big a noodle as the British girl is. You two make a good pair. Now go and help Kha in the kitchen!"

Sue Lin walked toward the kitchen, staring at her hand, a dreamy look on her face. Her mistress watched her go for a moment then sighed and chuckled. Presently she heard Kha asking Sue Lin what was wrong with her hand. That got another chuckle out of her.

4.

It was evening. A peacock's chatter echoed somewhere in the distance. The house was quiet and the great room was in shadows. Sen Loi sat at her desk working by the light of a lamp, going over receipts and bills concerning her gambling concession The Blue Dragon. She looked up as she heard a motorcycle out behind the garden. In a while she heard Pug come into the kitchen. He talked a moment with Sue Lin and Kha, then came into the great room and took a chair next to his mistress.

"Have you learned anything concerning the death of Chief Inspector Barnes?"

Pug nodded. "The rumor is that he was on the trail of some pirates and a certain barber."

Sen Loi turned in her chair to face her chauffeur. "Pirates? Barbers? That's an odd combination."

Pug chuckled. "Not when the pirate is Chung-zi and the barber is Yamaguchi."

Chung-zi, you say? My old enemy? The British have a sizeable reward out for his head?"

"Indeed! But he's still out there raiding their opium shipments from India."

Sen Loi smiled mischievously. "And my people raid his boats in return. He gets the blame and we get the goods. Justice is sweet, I always say."

"As long as the British don't catch on to us."

Sen Loi thought for a moment, and then said, "So, what is the pirate's connection with this barber?"

"Yamaguchi is bribing a clerk in a certain British import-export firm, here in Kowloon," Pug explained. "This clerk gives the barber information as to what British ships are bringing in opium, and also their routes of travel. The barber then sells this information to the pirate."

"And Inspector Barnes got wind of all this and Yamaguchi had him killed? Is that it?"

"Oh, no, the barber is too cautious for that. He got the pirate to do the dirty work."

"And the British want to hang me for it! Isn't that just sweet?"

"Well, it appears to be working mistress. You're their prime suspect, so far."

"According to Inspector Marion, I am their only suspect!"

There was a moment silence and then Pug said, "Sue Lin said the British girl was here today."

"Yes."

"How did it go?"

"It went well," Sen Loi said. "But there's something sad about her. She is naïve, and fate has played around with her. Do you know anything about her uncle?"

"He is well-known in the bistros and brothels of Kowloon. He's a night prowler, they say."

"Oh, really?" Sen Loi chuckled. "If that ever came to the attention of Lady St. John and her people, he would be finished."

"There is also a rumor going around that he is dipping into the girl's inheritance, to support his bad habits."

"Really? But why?"

"To pay for his carnal pleasures and gambling debts."

Sen Loi nodded again. "I never told her, but he has lost a considerable sum of money at the Blue Dragon in the past few weeks. We're holding several of his I.O.U's."

"Why are you concerned about her, mistress? She doesn't care about any of us. She lives in a different world."

"That is true, but today I saw a scared little girl who needs love and understanding. She was crying out for help. It was very sad to see."

"My advice is not to get involved with her, mistress. She will only bring you more trouble...and you have plenty of trouble right now." Pug sighed. "Anyway, she's British."

Suddenly Kha and Sue Lin came from the kitchen, jabbering at each other. They stopped next to Pug, staring over at Sen Loi.

"Tell them, grandmother!" Sue Lin said.

"Tell us what?" Pug asked.

"She had another dream."

Both Pug and Sen Loi chuckled. Pug winked at his mistress as if to say, "Oh, oh! Here it comes!"

Kha saw it and said, "Yes I did, and you had better not make fun of me!"

"Alright...what was it this time, little one?" Sen Loi asked with a big sigh.

"Well, an eagle swooped down on a mouse and the mouse turned into a cobra and killed the eagle!" Kha said with authority." And that's that!"

"And what's that supposed to mean?" Pug dared ask.

"It means awful trouble will fall upon our great house because of that *gueillo* girl! That's what it means!"

"Old one, I think you just like to tell tall tales," Sen Loi said.

"Oh, I'm telling tall tales, am I? Well, you'll see. And when it happens, don't say I didn't tell you!"

With that warning, Kha rushed back into the kitchen mumbling incoherently.

Sue Lin spoke up, "You shouldn't make her mad...she might spit in the food."

Pug shivered. "Now that's a nice thought."

"She just likes attention is all," Sen Loi said.

"Well, you don't want to get her pissed at you, mistress," Sue Lin said with authority.

"Pissed?" Pug chuckled. "Now there's a nice British word for you."

"Yes," Sen Loi said, "and you had better not use it again."

"Yes, mistress," Sue Lin said in a subdued voice.

Pug looked at Sue Lin and smirked, saying, "And you best not forget it, little mouse."

"Oh, shut up you, you gorilla!" Sue Lin said indignantly.

Pug burst out laughing.

Sue Lin turned to her mistress. "Mistress, when is Joan coming again, do you know?"

"No, I don't know. Maybe never. Why should she come here anyway? She got what she wanted, so she has no reason to come back."

Pug chuckled. "Sue Lin is in love with the British girl, aren't you, Sue Lin?"

"Oh, be quiet, you little man! Nobody asked you for your opinion!"

"Oh, little man am I, you little pigeon," Pug said. "Why, I could crush you with one finger. So you better be careful what you say to me!"

Suddenly the kitchen door opened and Kha stuck her head out.

"Pug! There's a cockroach in the yard asking to see you!" she growled.

"Who is it?"

"I don't know and I don't care!"

Pug got up and went through the kitchen and out into the herb garden.

Sen Loi looked at Sue Lin. "You shouldn't make Pug angry."

"Oh, he's just a great big pussycat. He wouldn't hurt me."

"Still, you should treat him with respect."

"Oh, alright, then," Sue Lin said. After a short pause, "Isn't Joan wonderful, mistress?"

"It's back to Joan, is it?" Sen Loi resumed her paper work. "Yes, she is wonderful, but also troubled, very troubled."

"Maybe we could help her."

"Oh and how do you propose we do that?"

"Ah, well, she could stay here, with us, couldn't she?"

"That's a ridiculous idea and quite impossible."

"Why is it impossible? You always said nothing is impossible, if you think about it," Sue Lin pouted.

"It's impossible because she's British. And for another thing, she lives with her uncle."

"That's true," Sue Lin said with a far look in her eyes. "But he could disappear, you know? He could go poof!"

"He won't go poof! Why would he go, poof?"

"People in Kowloon go poof every day, don't they?"

Sen Loi stopped her work and turned to her ward. "Are you talking about what I think you're talking about with this poof business?"

"Uh...maybe."

"Well, if it is, you are a bad, bad, little girl. Do you know that?"

"Yes, mistress, I suppose I am, but…"

"And I should send you back to the orphanage in Wu Han," Sen Loi said. "But on second thought that's not a good idea because you'd only corrupt everyone there. So I guess I'm stuck with you."

"Thank you mistress. You're too kind to lowly Sue Lin. I don't deserve a benefactor as kind as you."

"And don't try to butter me up. It won't work."

"No, mistress."

Pug came out of the kitchen, into the great room. He took his seat next to his mistress at the desk.

"Who was it?"

"One of the informants."

"Anything good?"

"I think so. It seems the girl's uncle gets his hair cut down in Shim Sha Tsui."

"And that is important, because?"

"Because that's where Yamaguchi has his barber shop, on Chatham Street. The uncle goes there as often as once a week, sometimes," Pug said.

"He must have very fast growing hair."

"It seems that your name comes up a lot."

"My name? I don't even know Joan's uncle, or his barber, for that matter!"

"Well, he has evidently heard of you, mistress."

"Wait! I know! It has to do with the girl. They all told her not come here." Sen Loi thought for a moment. "But, there must be more to it than that."

"It might be about the Blue Dragon, mistress. He might know that you are half owner."

"Yes, he is always there. He may have seen me and asked about me. He owes us quite a lot of money," Sen Loi said. "Anything else, my friend?"

"Yes. They say that when he drinks, he can get pretty rough with the girl."

Sen Loi looked concerned. "Do they say he puts his hands on her?"

"Sometimes, yes. They say he can go a little crazy, when drunk."

"If anything happens to Joan he would get all the money," Sen Loi said.

"Yes, every penny. The whole lot of it." Pug said.

Sue Lin suddenly came alive: "See? I told you he should go poof, didn't I?"

"Yes and perhaps he will, yet."

"Oh, one more thing, less I forget," Pug said ominously. "Some of Chung-zi's men have been spotted sneaking about the docks, lately."

Sen Loi's face clouded over. "Then he must be hiding nearby."

"Yes. And if so, then he and the barber are up to something."

Sen Loi chuckled. "He's got nerve. I'll give him that. And with the British Navy looking all over for him. What in the world can he be up to, Pug?"

"Personally I think he's after you, mistress, for raiding his ships. I really do."

"That's possible, but I think there is more to it than that, Pug," Sen Loi said. "But the only way to find out for sure is for you to get the informants digging into it."

"I already have, mistress," Pug replied. "And it won't be long before we know the answer."

"Good work, Pug," Sen Loi said.

Sen Loi opened a drawer and pulled out a big green ledger and resumed work. Sue Lin went over to a far corner where a Victrola sat on a tabouret. She put on a record and wound the starting arm and set it to playing. She walked in a sultry way over to Pug and grabbed his arm.

"Come, my Valentino, come dance with me!"

"Go away, little flea! Don't bother me!" Pug didn't budge.

"Come, take me, my Lothario! I am all yours!" She tugged hard at the big man's arm, to no effect.

Finally Sen Loi couldn't stand it any further. "Dance with the little beggar Pug, before she drive us both into the madhouse!"

Pug slowly got up and Sue Lin led him to an empty spot in the great room. He placed his arm around her tiny waist.

"Do you know the tango?" she asked.

"Never heard of it," Pug said.

But he had lied. He swept the tiny girl up, and in no time at all they were dancing passionately to "Tango of the Roses."

Sen Loi stopped working and looked on with a smile.

5.

During the passing week, Sen Loi spent her evenings at the Blue Dragon. Her partner, a very old man, was laid up at home with a severe cold that seemed to be widespread throughout the Kowloon area. The Chinese blamed the outbreak on the British, and the British blamed it on the French, and French blamed it on the Germans, and, they all called each other spies. The Japanese just stepped back and took a low profile.

By the end of the week her partner was in fit shape and back on the job. He listened sympathetically as Sen Loi told him about her problem with the British. He wisely advised her to go on hiatus and get it resolved, then return to work. She agreed.

One afternoon, the British girl paid Sen Loi and her household an unexpected but welcomed visit.

"Joan, how very nice to see you!" Sen Loi said. She immediately noticed that Joan was a bit crestfallen. The

British girl stood in the great room fidgeting with her handbag.

"I hope I'm not intruding, Madam Loi," the girl said sheepishly.

"Intruding? Nonsense, Joan. You're always welcome here. Come, sit." Joan sat down at the big table.

"Are you sure I'm not intruding? Perhaps I should go," Joan said nervously. She looked up at Sen Loi. "I just happened to be…"

"Passing by," Sen Loi said, "and you decided to drop in." Sen Loi sat at the table across from Joan.

"Is Sue Lin at home?" Joan asked, looking around.

"Yes, she is," Sen Loi said. She called loudly into the kitchen. "Sue Lin, Joan is here! Bring tea and cookies!"

"I don't want to be a bother, Madam Loi, Perhaps I shouldn't have come."

Sen Loi continued to study the young girl's face. "You look sad, Joan. Is something wrong?"

Joan looked away and sighed. "It's nothing, really."

"No Joan, no secrets between us. Tell me what's bothering you?"

"Well, the truth is, it's my Uncle Jack. He's been, well, very difficult, lately. We, uh, had a big fight."

"Oh? And, what was this big fight about?"

"It's been unbearable, lately. It's as if I'm his prisoner. I can't go here, or I can't go there." Joan paused to select the right words. "I have to practically beg for my allowance! He dominates me, and I hate that!"

"Does he put his hands on you?"

"No, but he did threaten to punish me, but he put his fist into the wall, instead." Joan shivered. "He's awfully strong."

"What about your friends, Lady St. John? Do they know what's going on?"

"No, I'm too embarrassed to bring it up. And well, I'm ashamed too, I suppose."

The girl's eyes moistened. She struggled to hold back tears. Sen Loi put a comforting hand on her shoulder. Finally, Joan looked up and said, "I'm sorry."

"There's nothing to be sorry about Joan. Where's your Uncle Jack now?"

"I have no idea. After we had the fight he stormed off raving mad. He'll stay out late and come back completely soused and mean. That's how he gets, when he drinks."

"Would you like to stay here, tonight, Joan? You can, if you wish."

The girl gave the offer some thought. "No. I'd best not. I just had to get away, to talk to someone."

"Of course you did, Joan."

Sue Lin came from the kitchen with a tray. A bottle of wine and three glasses were on it. She set it down on the table and uncorked the wine.

Sen Loi frowned at her saying, "This doesn't look like tea to me, young lady."

"Joan doesn't need tea right now," Sue Lin said as she poured the wine. "Isn't that right, Joan?"

Joan's face lit up. She smiled. "Come to think of it, perhaps I don't! Wine would be just fine!"

"See, mistress?" Sue Lin was beaming. "Am I not right?" She stood close to the British girl.

"Yes, yes, you are always right, you silly, little goose!" Sen Loi admitted.

They all laughed and took up their glasses. "A toast to the Debutante of Kowloon…Miss Joan Wainwright!" Sue Lin said loudly. They touched glasses. And sipped the wine.

"I didn't know the Chinese made real wine."

"Oh, yes," Sen Loi said. "Our grape wines date back almost five-thousand years, Joan."

"Oh, really? What is this one called?"

"It is called *huang-jiu*. The Americans call it, '*yellow wine*.'"

Joan took another sip. "It is rather strong, isn't it?"

"Yes. It is stronger than *chang-yu*, or *chang-yu-Jie Bay Na*, which is a cabernet that has the flavor of pepper and black currants. You should try those sometime, Joan. I'm sure you would like them."

"Well, actually I'm not much of a drinker," Joan said. "But I really like this *huang-jiu*!"

Sue Lin raised her glass again. "To the most beautiful British girl in Kowloon, Joan Wainwright!" Joan and Sue Lin sipped more wine. Sen Loi looked on, amused.

"Oh, this wine is really delicious," Joan said in a dreamy, relaxed voice.

"Yes," Sue Lin said, "but not as delicious as Joan Wainwright!"

Joan's eyes widened and she smiled. "What was that?"

Sen Loi cut in. "Pay no attention to her, Joan. She's is sometimes what we Chinese call, 'dingy-dingy.'"

"Dingy-dingy?"

"Yes, nippy-nippy."

"I don't…" Joan stared to say.

"My mistress is telling you that sometimes I act a bit strange," Sue Lin said.

"Oh, you mean, you're sometime nutty!"

"Yes. I'm sometimes nutty!" The two young girls giggled.

Joan finally said, "If you're nutty, then you had better watch out for the squirrels, Sue Lin!" They resumed laughing loud and long.

Sen Loi scowled at Sue Lin. "I don't think this wine is such a very good idea, young lady."

"Trust me, mistress," Sue Lin said, trying to get control of herself, holding her side. "Joan needs this."

Joan nodded. "Come to think of it, I guess I do. Thank you, Sue Lin, you dear, dear friend!"

Sue Lin, still standing next to Joan, smiled down at her. "You're welcome, Joan Wainwright. Joan Wainwright! What a beautiful name!"

Sen Loi made an attempt to slow things down a bit. "You're parents, Joan, I imagine you miss them terribly."

Joan thought that over and giggled. "To be truthful ma'am, I have spent most of my life away from them. In and out of one finishing school after another. I was a rather difficult child."

Sue Lin said, "Gee, I bet that was fun!" She refilled both their glasses.

"I don't know," Joan said laughingly. "I never finished finishing school, so I can't say!"

This sent the two young girls out of control again, giggling and twitching.

"But, you must have learned something of value, Joan, didn't you?" Sen Loi was trying to sober things up.

Joan took another sip of wine. "Well, that depends what you call value. I learned to be well read and be polite and proper, and behave in the company of 'hoity-toity' people."

Sue Lin said, "But you're not 'hoity-toity,' are you, Joan?"

"Who, me? Oh, dear me, no! I just could never take to acting 'hoity-toity,' and snooty." The British girl said with a chuckle.

Sue Lin pointed at Sen Loi. "But Mistress is all 'hoity-toity,' and snooty, right Mistress?"

"Sue Lin! Did you put something in this wine, you little rascal?"

Sue Lin snickered mischievously. "Who, me Mistress? No, but perhaps Kha did!" Sue Lin topped off hers and

Joan's glasses. "Forgive me for asking, Joan or maybe I shouldn't?"

Sen Loi interrupted. "No, Sue Lin. Whatever it is, no!"

"Heck, girl! Just bring it up! No matter what it is, just bring it the heck up!" Joan said her voice thick from too much wine.

Sue Lin continued. "Well, I read in the Society Column that you and Bobby St. John broke up. Is that true, Joan?"

Joan suddenly frowned. She began sobbing. "Yes, it's true. He dumped me. Just like that!" She tried to snap her fingers but couldn't quite get them to work.

Sue Lin tried it. "You mean like this?" Her fingers didn't seem to work, either. "Never mind. I know what you mean."

"Perhaps Joan doesn't want to talk about it, Sue Lin," Sen Loi said.

Joan stopped sobbing. A look of determination came over her face. "Bobby St. John can go jump in the lake, for all I care. After all, I have my pride, don't I, huh?"

"Well, of course you do, Joan," Sen Loi said soothingly.

"Oh, he'll come back, Joan," Sue Lin sneered. "He'll come crawling back on his knees, through a field of broken glass, in the freezing cold, with frozen lips begging for forgiveness! But don't you take him back, Joan! No! You spit on him! You kick him!"

"Sue Lin! That's enough!"

Suddenly Sue Lin looked very shy and innocent. "Yes, Mistress?"

Sen Loi searched her brain for a more calming subject. "Joan, how are your rescued horses doing these days?"

"Oh," Joan said calmly. "They're doing very well, Madam Loi, thank you."

"Getting fat and lazy, are they?"

"Yep! Fat and lazy."

Sue Lin saw an opening and took it. "Ah, do you provide mares for them, Joan?"

The British girl was taken by surprise for a moment. "Mares? No. Why do you ask?"

"Well, think about it, Joan," Sue Lin said in a matter-of-fact manner. "If you were a mare, would you like to spend the rest of your life without a stallion?"

"Well, I…"

"Oh, look, Mistress "I have made Joan blush!"

"I should have warned you about Sue Lin, Joan," Sen Loi said. "She has no shame."

Joan smiled. "Oh, I don't mind." For a moment she looked sober. She looked about the room and sighed. "It's so peaceful here. So quiet. I just love it here. It feels so safe."

"Safety can be a temporary condition. One never knows when it will change. So you must be careful. There is danger all around you, Joan."

"Oh, I'm fine, Madam Loi. I'm fine and Sue Lin is fine and you're fine." Suddenly the girl made a big yawn. "Oh, dear me. Suddenly I feel very sleepy. Perhaps I'm too relaxed."

Sue Lin put down her glass and bent forward and kissed the British girl lightly on the mouth. Joan giggled and pushed her away.

"You naughty Chinese girl, I should spank for doing that!"

"You need a good spanking yourself, you British girl!"

"Alright! Let's spank each other! Me, first!"

The two girls laughed hard. Suddenly Joan stopped and stood up with a blank look. Her face had suddenly gone pale. Sen Loi quickly rose, also.

"Joan, are you alright?" Sen Loi asked.

"Oh, gosh! I think I'm going to be ill." Joan quickly put a hand over her mouth.

Sen Loi barked at Sue Lin, "Quick! Take Joan into the kitchen!"

Sue Lin grabbed Joan's free hand and pulled her along to the kitchen. A moment later Pug came out with a puzzled look on his face.

"What's going on, Mistress? The British girl is throwing up in the kitchen sink!"

"That little stinker Sue Lin has gotten her drunk on *huang-yui*."

"I guess she's the champagne type, huh?" Pug said laughing.

"Apparently so."

"How did she get here?"

"I have no idea. Most likely a taxi."

Pug went and looked out front. "Well, it's gone. Nothing is out there."

"Then I guess you'll have to take her home."

"Sure, if you want me to."

"But try not to be seen. Is it dark out yet?"

"Almost. By the time I get her home, it will be."

"Good. But be as discrete as possible. And avoid the British. But make sure she gets home safe."

Moments later, Sue Lin led a wobbly Joan Wainwright out of the kitchen.

"Joan is feeling better now, Mistress. Kha gave her a tonic to settle her stomach."

"I'm so sorry, Madam Loi. I'm so embarrassed."

"Don't be, Joan. Are you alright now?"

"Yes, I think so."

"I think you haven't been eating properly or getting enough sleep these past few weeks, have you?"

"No, I'm afraid I haven't."

"You must go home and rest. Pug will see that you get there safely, won't you Pug?" Pug nodded.

"Thank you, but I have a taxi outside. I paid him to wait."

"He must have misunderstood you, Joan. He's gone now."

Sue Lin handed Joan her handbag. She entwined the girl's arm in her own and led her outside to the Bentley. Sen Loi followed.

"Be careful, Pug," Sen Loi said. The evening was now cool and the sun was red on the horizon.

"Don't worry so much," Pug said as he started the car and drove slowly away.

Sen Loi watched the Bentley go out of sight. She had a worried look on her face.

6.

It was early morning the following day, and Sen Loi sat at her desk with a blank look on her face. She stared down at the pile of paperwork in front of her. She sighed and turned in her chair just as Sue Lin and Kha came out of the kitchen. They had been up all night, waiting for Pug to return.

"He's dead," Sue Lin sobbed. "They killed him! I just know they did!"

"I had a dream last night," the old one said. "Ghosts were walking the streets of Kowloon, and it was raining blood!"

"What is that supposed to mean, grandmother?" Sen Loi asked. Kha was waiting and ready for that very question.

"It means that the war up north will soon come here, and it will be very bad for us," the old lady growled.

Sue Lin asked, "What has that got to do with Pug not coming home?"

"I'm not talking about him. I'm talking about us, that's who I'm talking about!" Kha said.

Sue Lin sighed. "Poor Pug! I'll never see his ugly face again! Oh, I just love that face!"

Sen Loi chuckled. "Sue Lin you're a drama queen, you know that?"

Sue Lin ignored the criticism. "Maybe we should notify what's-his-name? That handsome British policeman?"

"Inspector Marion?" Sen Loi sneered. "Well, of course we should. Then he can accuse me of murdering my own chauffeur."

Sue Lin held a hand across her brow, like a silent movie star. "Oh, Pug! Dear, dear Pug! I love you dear friend!"

"And I love you, too, little bird!"

The voice came from the kitchen and a moment later Pug came wobbling into the great room, unsteady on his feet. He sat down by the desk, next to his mistress. His face was bruised and his uniform was wrinkled and covered with mud. He slumped into the chair and groaned in pain.

"You're hurt!" Sen Loi cried. She put an arm on the giant's shoulder. "Do you need a doctor?"

"I'm alright, but they got the girl," Pug said in a rasping voice. He gasped for air.

There was a moment of stunned silence. "Who got her?" Sen Loi asked.

Pug groaned and rubbed his neck. "I'm not sure who they were. It was too dark to see much. They attacked me in front of her place, just as I got out of the car."

"It was her uncle!" Sue Lin hissed. "The rat hired some thugs to jump you and take her!"

Kha went quickly into the kitchen, saying. "He needs a stiff drink."

"They wore masks. I did my best but there were too many, mistress. Forgive me."

"There is nothing to forgive. The main thing is you're alive. And I'm sure Joan is, too."

Kha came back with a shot of brandy. Pug took it all down in one swallow and handed her the empty glass.

"Did they smell?" Kha asked him.

"What?" Pug asked.

"Did they smell? Like the sea. Like salted fish?"

"Come to think of it, yes! They really stank of it!"

Kha nodded. "They were Chung-zi's assassins from the Cobra Triad. Their bodies are all covered with green snake tattoos. They know each other in the dark by their smell. "You're lucky to be alive!"

"So, they overpowered you and took Joan." Sen Loi said. "But why were you gone all night?"

"They knocked me out and when I woke up I was in the woods, up in the Lo Wu district. They took Joan and the car. I had to beg a ride back here." Pug explained. "Get me another brandy, please, grandmother."

"No, what you need is a hot bath and rest!"

"Poor, poor Joan!" Sue Lin sighed deeply. "It's good she was drunk when this happened, right, mistress?"

"No, it is not good! She will need to have all her wits about her, to think clearly," Sen Loi said.

"Well, at least she's alive, right?"

Pug cut in. "Yes, if indeed she is alive. But soon she may be wishing she was dead, when the pirates get through with her."

Sue Lin eyes widened. "But what will they do to her?"

Pug looked at Sue Lin. "Rape, torture, drugs. A whole bunch of nice things."

"That is, unless Chung-zi has a special plan for her," Sen Loi said.

"A special plan, mistress?" Sue Lin asked.

"If he decides to sell her into slavery, a girl such as Joan would bring a fortune."

Kha shook her head. "That would surely be worse than death for the British girl."

Sen Loi nodded. "Yes. They will keep her drugged on opium, day and night. Over time she will age quickly. Her body will waste away."

"Oh, mistress! Can't you do something? Can't you save her?"

"No," Sen Loi said.

"Joan!" Sue Lin cried out dramatically. "Oh, dear, dear Joan."

"Oh, be quiet, little snail!" Pug said. "This isn't an audition for a movie!"

"Unless…" Sen Loi paused.

Kha froze in place and stared at Sen Loi. "Oh, no! Don't even think it! Let the British take care of it!"

"Unless what?" Sue Lin urged her mistress on.

"Unless we…"

Suddenly a car pulled up in front of the house. Doors opened and slammed shut. Footsteps pounded the gravel in the courtyard. Then someone pounded angrily on the door.

"Open up! Police!" It was Inspector Marion.

Sen Loi quickly got up and pointed. "Quick, Pug! Get behind the books!"

Pug ran over to the bookcase that stood against the wall, facing the kitchen. He grabbed it by one corner, swung it open like a door, and stepped into a recess behind it. Su Lin quickly pushed it shut.

"Go, quickly!" Sen Loi said. Kha and Sue Lin went into the kitchen.

Sen Loi composed herself then went slowly into the foyer to open the front door and admit Inspector Marion. He rushed boldly past her, to the entrance of the great room. He looked around, his eyes blazing.

"Don't anyone move! I have the house surrounded!" the Inspector cried out.

Sen Loi turned to face him. "Inspector Marion! How nice to see you again! What brings you to my humble home so early in the day?"

"Don't play innocent with me, madam!" The Inspector was spitting-mad. "You know full well why I am here!" He glared at her.

Sen Loi pretended to be surprised. "But I really don't, Inspector."

"Where is he?" the Inspector shouted.

"Where is who sir?" Sen Loi looked around, waving her arm. "There is no one here except you and me."

"Your driver! Where is he?"

"You mean Pug? Oh, he isn't here."

"I could get a search warrant, you know," the Inspector growled. "I'll tear this place apart, if I do!"

Sen Loi came up close to Marion. "Why are you so interested in him, Inspector?"

"I'm taking him in for suspicion of kidnapping. That's all you need to know, madam."

Sen Loi walked into the great room, to the dining table. "To be truthful, I too was wondering where he is. You see, he took a guest of mine home last night, and I haven't seen him since."

The Inspector followed Sen Loi into the great room, an intensive look on his face. "Was that guest, by any chance, a British girl? A Miss Joan Wainwright?"

"Why, yes! How did you know, Inspector?"

"Because, late last night her uncle reported her missing!"

"But she left here before dark, Inspector."

"And now she's missing."

"And so is my driver and car," Sen Loi said. "You are free to search my home, inspector, if it pleases you. But it will be a waste of time, I assure you. You won't find him."

"Oh, I'll find him, rest assured of that madam."

"Well, I sincerely hope you do. Actually I never trusted him. He was sneaky and lazy. I should have fired him a long time ago. Do you really think he kidnapped Miss Wainwright?"

"Oh, there's no doubt about that, madam!"

"I hear that the pirate Chung-zi is in the area. Do you think there is a connection there?"

"Chung-zi, did you say?" The policeman paused to think. His face brightened. "Why yes! That makes sense! Ransom! Yes, that's the motive! Ransom! The Wainwright girl is worth a fortune!"

"So you think Pug either sold the British girl to the pirates or he joined that gang of cutthroats for a piece of the ransom?"

The Inspector stroked his chin and pondered the possibilities. "Yes. That is possible, isn't it?"

"Then he must be caught!" Sen Loi said. "If I were you, Inspector, I would get on the trail right away. I would start by finding my Bentley. Look for clues, you know. Footprints and that sort of thing."

"Good thinking, madam!" the Inspector said enthusiastically. He started to leave. Suddenly, at the door, he stopped. He chuckled and turned to Sen Loi. "Nice try, madam, but it won't work."

"Whatever do you mean, Inspector?"

"I mean your pitiful attempt to get me out of the way."

"But I assure you, I'm attempting no such thing. Stay as long as you wish. Make your search, if you want. By all means, please do."

The Inspector suddenly seemed a bit unsure of his next move. "Perhaps later…but in the meantime, you are not to leave this house."

"Oh? Am I under house arrest, Inspector?"

"Yes, madam, you are. I'm going to get a judgment against you, so consider it in effect as of now," the Inspector said. "You haven't fooled me one bit." He paused. "And I still think you had a hand in the death of Chief Inspector Barnes, as well as in the disappearance of the Wainwright girl."

"He spoke highly of you, you know?"

"Who spoke highly of me?"

"The Chief Inspector. He said you were a rising star in the Service."

Marion sneered. "What gibberish! He hardly noticed me."

"You are deeply mistaken there, Inspector. He said you were smart and thorough. He had his eye on you to replace him, when he retired."

"Well, if he did, he never let on."

"No, he wouldn't. He was the quiet, observing type. But he did admire you."

Marion blinked several times and cleared his throat, his eyes glassing over a bit. "Not as much as I admired him, the old codger! He's a legend, he is."

"It's a pity you two never got to work together. Barnes and Marion, side-by-side. What a team that would have made."

The young Inspector looked away. He blinked back tears and cleared his throat. "I appreciate you telling me all this, madam. He never did let me know how he felt about me. I thought he disliked me, for some reason. He was always rather harsh with me, but I suppose that was his way."

"Yes. He was hard as nails on the outside, but considerate and human on the inside."

There was a moment of quiet. "Yes, well, alright. I'll have my men search for your car. Get it back to you. Do I have your word that you will remain here, on the premises? That you will not leave your house?"

"You have my word, Inspector."

"Rest assured, I shall hold you to it, madam," the Inspector said.

He looked around for a second time, nodded, went through the foyer and left. A few moments later there was the sound of voices. Feet sounded on the gravel in the courtyard. Car doors opened and closed. Engines started up and the cars left.

Sen Loi went into the kitchen.

"What a knucklehead," Sue Lin said. "He's handsome, but stupid."

Kha chuckled. "You sure did a con job on him."

"You two have been going to too many American movies," Sen Loi chuckled. "I'll have to put a stop to that."

"That stuff you gave him about the Chief Inspector Barnes. It was a big lie. Barnes thought he was an idiot," Kha said. "I heard him say that many times while you two were playing chess."

"As did I," Sue Lin said. "He also said Inspector Marion was as dumb as wood!"

Sen Loi frowned "Yes, but I couldn't very well tell him that, could I?"

Suddenly they heard Pug coming out of the bookcase. He came into the kitchen grumbling.

"Going to leave me in there all day, were you?"

Sue Lin gave him a big hug. He quickly mellowed.

"Pug, my friend," Sen Loi said, "you shall eat, take a bath, and sleep. Then, tonight, you will go out on a mission. Are you up to it?"

"Sure," Pug said. "What do you have in mind?"

"Around mid-night, you'll get the motorcycle from the shed out back and put the side car on it."

"Then what?"

"Then go to the home of the barber Yamaguchi, gag him, tie him up, and bring him back here."

"The barber? Why the barber, mistress? Do you think he had something to do with the girl's disappearance?" Sue Lin asked.

"I think all things are connected, the barber, the pirate, and the uncle."

"Are you sure, Mistress?"

"Right now, no. But when I'm finished with the barber we will know a little more. Maybe enough to save the girl," Sen Loi said.

"I don't think the barber will talk, mistress," Pug said. "He's a real slick operator and pretty tough."

"In that case we might have to use the green box."

Kha nodded in agreement. "Then, I'll have it ready," she said.

7.

It was just after mid-night. Sen Loi was at her desk going over paperwork by the light of a desk lamp. Sue Lin sat at the dining table reading a newspaper under a white cone of light that shone down above her head. Kha came in from the kitchen.

"Do you want something? Maybe tea?" she asked Sen Loi.

"No. Perhaps later, thank you."

Kha went back into the kitchen. Sue Lin put down the paper and went over and sat in a chair by her mistress. Sen Loi ignored her.

"I can't read anymore. I'm too worried about Pug. Poor man, you work him to death."

"Oh, I think her enjoys it well enough." Sen Loi kept working. "If he didn't, he would have moved on a long time ago."

"Where did you find him, mistress?"

"I didn't, he found me."

"Oh, how?"

"I'm in no mood for idle chit-chat right now, so don't bother me."

"Please? Pretty please?"

Sen Loi turned to face the girl. "Oh, alright, you little pest. Then leave me to my work."

"Oh, goody-goody! I'm listening!"

Sen Loi put her pen down and paused a moment to think about where to begin the story. She finally started.

"Many years ago, as I was leaving Mother China for the Colony, my car broke down on the Guangdong Road. My mother, who had been my father's first wife, had just died, and I was coming to find my father here in Kowloon."

"I'm sorry to hear your mother died, mistress."

"Thank you. As I said, my car broke down on a lonely stretch of road miles from Guangdong. When my driver got out to change the wheel, three bandits came out of the woods to attack us."

"Oh, that wasn't good."

"No, indeed. One killed my driver instantly, and the other two pulled me from the car and laid me over the hood."

"What for? To rob you?"

"No, little one, to rape me. They pulled down their pantaloons for that very purpose, leaving their bare backsides hanging in the wind," Sue Lin giggled and held a hand over her mouth, trying to stop. "You find that funny?"

"I'm sorry, mistress, but the vision of three bare behinds hanging in the wind has tickled my funny-bone. Please go on. Did they?"

"Rape me? No, but they were just about to, and would have, had not a big, bald giant, dressed in rags, come whistling down the road in our direction. He stopped and calmly asked them what they were doing?"

"And that was Pug! Right?"

"Indeed it was."

"Oh, please go on mistress!"

"Well, the leader of these three cutthroats told Pug to go about his business or they would give him plenty of trouble, if he didn't. I screamed at him not to go. They said, 'go!' and I screamed, 'stay!'"

"Oh, gee, then, what?"

"Well, Pug asked me where I was going, and I said Kowloon. Then he asked me, 'Do you need a new driver?' He looked down at my driver who lay in a pool of blood, his throat cut from ear-to-ear. 'Yes,' I said, 'You're hired. I will pay you well.'"

"What did Pug do then?"

"He broke the neck of one of the bandits and the other two ran off into the woods. Pug finished changing the wheel. We buried my dead driver by the side of the road, and we went on our way."

"Gosh!" Sue Lin said as if paying homage to a hero. "And that was our Pug?"

"Yes, that was our Pug."

"Did he tell you where he came from? Or anything about his life?"

"No, and I never asked. In fact, I don't even know his real name. I just call him Pug because it suits him."

Sue Lin chuckled, and then fell quiet. She sighed. Just as Sen Loi was about to return to her work, Sue Lin asked, "How about Kha? Where did she come from?"

"Kha? Well, that's a different story."

"Is she your mother or grandmother? You call her both, sometimes."

"I only use that as a manner of speaking. She is, was, my father's mother."

"Your grandmother?"

"Yes, my grandmother."

"And your father?"

"Dead."

"Then you are an orphan, just like me?"

"You could say that, yes, sort of."

"Why did you buy me from the orphanage, mistress?"

"Buy you? Why, they practically paid me to take you off their hands! You acted like a wild animal."

"I hated that place. My parents were peasant farmers. The last thing they wanted was a girl, so they sold me to the orphanage. I was so happy you took me out of there."

"If you don't behave, I'll put you right back there, little frog!"

Suddenly Su Lin rose quickly from the chair. "Listen!"

Kha came out and held the kitchen door wide open.

"Pug is here and he's carrying a sack of horse manure!" the old one snickered.

The big man came through the kitchen into the great room with the body of the barber over his right shoulder. The man's hands were tied behind his back and he was gagged and blindfolded. He kicked and squirmed to get free.

"Where do you want it, mistress?" Pug asked.

Sen Loi pointed. "There, at the table."

Pug placed the man in a standing position next to the dining room table and removed the blindfold and gag.

The barber gasped for air and screamed, "Help! Police!"

Pug untied Yamaguchi's hands and shoved him into a chair at the table.

Sen Loi stared at Yamaguchi. The barber had a large, oval-shaped head with thick black hair that was strewn wildly about his head. Large dark eyes bulged out from their sockets, above a big mouth with fat lips. His skin was very pale, and he glared like a trapped animal across the table at Sen Loi.

"What is the meaning of this?" the man growled. "I have government immunity! So you had better release me before you get into big, big trouble! Do you hear me?"

"I apologize for the inconvenience, Mr. Yamaguchi, but I really do need to ask you a few questions."

"Ask me some questions? Whoever you are, madam, you don't get to ask me any questions. I'm above the law! I have immunity! Help! Police!"

Kha turned to Sen Loi. "I think I should get the little green box, don't you?" Sen Loi nodded and Kha went into the kitchen.

Yamaguchi continued yelling. "Whoever you are, you silly Chinese person, you are in deep trouble here! I can tell you that!"

"Mr. Yamaguchi, if you would just calm down and cooperate, we can get this over with, and you can go back to your home unharmed."

That last word got the barber's attention. "Harm? How dare you threaten me, madam!"

"Yes, I know, you have immunity. But I'm afraid it is of no use to you here and now, Mr. Yamaguchi," Sen Loi said with faux sympathy.

Kha came from the kitchen carrying a small green box. It had a sliding partition in the middle that could be raised and lowered. At one end it had a round hole cut into it. She set it on the table with the hole facing the barber.

"What's that stupid thing?" Yamaguchi said, staring down at the box. "What's that for?"

"In my country, in ancient times, they called this the box of truth," Sen Loi said.

"Well, I don't care what they called the stupid thing," the barber said. "It doesn't scare me."

Sue Lin said, "Should I slap him, mistress?"

"No, we must have patience. I'm sure Mr. Yamaguchi will soon learn how to watch his tongue."

Sue Lin continued. "Well, I think he's bluffing. I think he's so afraid he's about to wet his pants. Isn't that so, Mr. Yamaguchi?"

"Oh, shut up you foolish girl!" The barber exploded in anger. "I'm not afraid of any of you. If that big, ugly giant wasn't here, I would thrash you all within an inch of your lives!"

"You have no reason to be afraid, sir," Sen Loi said, "if you will just be calm for a few moments and answer a few questions."

The barber sighed impatiently. "Oh, go on then, ask your stupid questions! Well? What are you waiting for? Huh? Huh? Ask! Ask!" Mr. Yamaguchi giggled nervously.

Sen Loi smiled. "Very good. Now you're being reasonable, sir. My question to you is who killed Chief Inspector Barnes and where is the British girl?"

"That's two questions."

"You're being very difficult," Sen Loi said. "I'll ask again, who killed the Chief Inspector and where is the British girl?"

"How should I know? I know nothing of such matters. I'm only a simple barber. I don't know anything about an Inspector or a British girl. What British girl?"

"It appears you know her uncle quite well. Do you not?"

"Her uncle? Oh, that man? Yes, he may have visited my shop once in a while. But I don't know him."

"Yet, you and the uncle mention my name quite often. Do you not?"

"You flatter yourself, madam. Why would I do that?" The barber smiled nervously and giggled again.

"Perhaps you have a close friend who, shall we say, wants me out of the way for good?"

"A friend of mine wants you out of the way? That's ridiculous!" Then, cautiously, "Just who is this friend of mine who wants you out of the way, madam?"

"Shall we say, Chung-zi, the pirate?"

Yamaguchi laughed a horrible, high-pitched laugh. He kept it going for a long time until he almost ran out of breath. He gasped for air, saying, "Oh, dear, I'm crying for laughing so hard! Chung-zi, you say? Why you're as crazy as a loon!" He suddenly turned nasty and sneered. "You had better let me go, madam. My absence will be reported to the police, and they will come looking for me. They will look everywhere. Kowloon will be flooded with police. A hurricane of police will descend on this house like a plague of locusts! You had all best surrender to me now, and I will go easy on you! Otherwise, you are all going to hang!"

Pug sighed. "This is getting us nowhere, mistress. I think it's time for the box."

"I fear you are right, my friend."

Sen Loi pushed the little green box closer to the barber. He stared down at it, a look of uncertainty on his face.

"Mr. Yamaguchi," Sen Loi said quietly but seriously, "I have been very civil here and what do you do? You insult me and my friends. What happens next will fall squarely on your shoulders." She pushed the green box closer to the barber.

"Why do you keep doing that?" the barber giggled nervously again. "What's that stupid thing for, anyway?"

"Let me explain exactly how the box works, Mr. Yamaguchi," Sen Loi said, "and then you can decide to answer my questions or not to answer my questions. The choice will be all yours."

Sue Lin whined, "We're wasting time, mistress! We must find Joan quickly! Let's just do it!"

"No, no, my child, we must follow protocol," Sen Loi said calmly as she looked at the barber. "Mr. Yamaguchi, do you see the hole there, in the box, facing you?"

"Of course I do, I'm not blind." The Barber yawned, pretending to be bored.

"Good, now do you see this pull up partition?" Sen Loi pointed to the partition.

"Yes, yes, yes! This is all very boring, you know. But do go on, if you must."

"Thank you," Sen Loi said lightly, with a smile. "Now, perhaps you would not be so bored if I told you that there is a bamboo viper on the other side of the pull up partition?"

"Oh, sure," Yamaguchi sneered. "A bamboo viper! Ha! You're trying to scare me. Well, it won't work. I well know it's just a bluff!"

Sen Loi leaned over the table and rapped the top of the green box with her hand. There was a sudden hissing sound and the box moved as something inside was thrashing angrily around behind the partition.

Suddenly the barber's eyes flared wide open and he jumped up from his chair.

"You barbarian! You heathen! You savage!" Yamaguchi screamed as he lunged to get free of Pug's grip.

Pug forced the barber down onto the chair. Sue Lin grabbed the barber's right hand, forcing it up to the hole in the box.

"You cretins!" Yamaguchi screamed. "I'll destroy you all!" He continued screaming until Pug slipped a hand over his mouth to shut him up.

"I'll count to five," Sen Loi said. "If you don't answer the questions you will die a most painful death."

Yamaguchi shook his head violently. Pug pulled his hand away from the barber's face. The barber began to sob.

"Alright, alright!" Tears rolled down his face. "Don't hurt me. I'll tell you anything you want to know."

"Who killed Chief Inspector Barnes?"

"It was the pirate. I had nothing to do with it."

"You had everything to do with it!" Sen Loi growled. "But let's move on. Where is the British girl?"

"Chung-zi has her."

"Where is he taking her?"

"To Shek-Kwu Island. He intends to sell her to the slavers who meet there."

"Why did he have the Chief Inspector murdered?"

"Because he found out about the clerk at the Kowloon Import-Export Company."

"Oh yes, the clerk you were bribing with Chung-zi's money."

The barber wiped away his tears and sniffed. "Look, I'm just an honest Kowloon businessman trying to make a living."

"Oh, of course, you are," Sen Loi sneered. "All you did was conspire to murder a British Police Inspector, kidnap a British girl, and frame me for both crimes!"

"Kidnaping the girl was the uncle's idea, not mine!" the barber said. "He's after her money. He wants to pay off his gambling and brothel debts."

"And how much did he promise you?" Sen Loi asked scornfully.

The barber hesitated for a moment. "Five hundred pounds, that's all." There was a moment of silence. "Can I go now? You promised."

"Yes, but first I want you to write it all down, every detail, just as you told it."

"No! I answered your dumb questions, so let me go! You promised!"

"Kha, go get the pen and paper."

"No, I won't! I gave you all I'm going to give you, you dishonest person!"

"Do you want me to count to five?" Sen Loi said seriously.

Yamaguchi whined. "Help me out here! Give me something, please!"

"I'm giving more than you deserve, Mr. Yamaguchi. More than you gave the Chief Inspector and the girl. They did nothing to you and look what they got? Did you give them something? You're lucky that I'm not going to kill you and dump your wretched body in the bay."

"Oh, alright! You coldhearted woman!"

Kha came over with an inkpot, pen, and several sheets of paper and set it all in front of the barber. Pug released him and reached into his own uniform jacket and pulled out some folded papers that had writing on them. He handed them to Sen Loi.

"What's this?" she asked.

"When I got to his house, he was up in his bedroom, in the closet, on a wireless radio, sending messages to someone. He tried to destroy this paperwork, but I got it first."

Sen Loi looked the papers over. "Very interesting. The names of British naval vessels in the area, the number of British troops stationed here in Kowloon, and much other information."

"Oh, my," Sue Lin said, She whistled softly. "Our Mr. Yamaguchi is a spy!"

"Who isn't?" Yamaguchi said. "We're all spies, aren't we?" He continued writing.

When he had completed the confession, Sen Loi looked it over. "Very well done, sir! Now you can go."

She looked over to Pug and nodded. He quickly grabbed the barber and began to tie his hands behind his back, and gag and blindfold him again. The barber started to struggle but finally gave up and let it happen. When Pug finished, Sen Loi took him aside.

"After you take Mr. Yamaguchi home, I want you to go and find Bobby St. John," she whispered.

"Lieutenant St. John? The British girl's fiancé? Or once fiancé? Why?"

"He is an officer in the Coast Guard, and he commands a British gunship that patrols the waters around Kowloon and Hong Kong Harbor. He's been after Chung-zi, so we'll make it a little easier for him to succeed."

"But, what do you want me to do, spank him, kiss him, or what?"

"Bring him here one way or another. But don't rough him up too much. I know I'm asking the impossible, but it's the only way to save the girl."

"I don't know, mistress. It won't be easy." And then, "With bruises or without?"

"Without, if possible, but if not, then with. But just get him here tonight. At this hour he may be home in bed or he may be at some nightclub. You may need help from your informants."

"Kowloon's not all that big. They'll know, alright," Pug said. "I'll do my best, mistress. This is a new one for me."

"And me," Sen Loi sighed. "But whether the girl lives or dies will depend on you, Pug."

Pug chuckled. "Gee, thanks, mistress. No pressure there, right?" He paused again. "In any case, Bobby St. John is as good as here."

"That's what I wanted to hear, my friend. Now, go."

Pug went over to the barber and slung him over his shoulder and disappeared though the kitchen. A few moments later they heard the bark and hum of the motorcycle as it sped away into the night.

Kha said, "Pleasant dreams barber."

8.

Sen Loi checked her watch. It was almost two-thirty in the morning. She paced the floor of the great room as she waited for Pug's return. Sue Lin came from the kitchen with a tray of tea and sandwiches and set it on the table.

"You had better eat, mistress."

"Just leave it."

"Pug's been gone over two hours, now. Do you think he ran into trouble?"

"He can take care of himself. Rest assured of that." Sen Loi said. She didn't sound too sure.

Sue Lin sat at the table and poured tea for them both. She took up a sandwich and began nibbling on it then put it down.

"You never talk about your father, mistress. Neither does Kha."

"No, we don't."

"I always wondered how you came into all this. The house, the Blue Dragon, and your money."

"I suppose you're thinking this was given to me, and that my father loved me and was kind to me. Is that what you think?" Sen Loi said, sitting down at the table, facing Sue Lin.

"Well, yes, that's what I'd like to think."

"Well, you'd be thinking wrong. My father was a cruel and ruthless man. He was the head of a triad called, 'The Green Crescent Moon Assassins.' He was a murderer. In his day, the triads ruled Kowloon."

"But he loved you, didn't he?"

"No, he did not."

"Oh, what happened when you and Pug arrived here from Guangdong? You never finished that story."

Sen Loi collected her thoughts for a moment.

"Well, when we got here I was lost. Lucky for me Pug had been here before and knew some people who put us on to my father. He was surprised to see me. When I told him his first wife, my mother, had died, he shrugged it off as if he didn't even know her. He had three concubines living in the house."

"And Kha, his mother, too, right?"

"Yes. Kha was also here."

"The concubines, did they give you trouble?"

"Oh, they tried, and would have run me off, too, had it not been for Kha. She and my mother had once been friends, so she kept me safe from the concubines. Lucky for me, none of them had any children. He wouldn't have allowed it, anyway."

"That meant you were the only true heir."

"Yes and because of that, my father tried various ways to get rid of me. He tried bribery, he beat me, and finally he tried to poison me. He also tried to get rid of Pug, but Kha liked Pug and hid him away."

"Your father did this?"

"Yes."

"How did you manage to survive?"

"Kha saved me."

"How?"

"As you know, Kha is an excellent herbalist. When she saw I was sick from the poison my father arranged to put in my food, she gave me a purgative and got it quickly out of my body."

"Where is your father now?"

"Gone. He got what he deserved."

"Oh, how? What happened?"

"What happened? Well, my father had a lot of enemies in Kowloon. He kept a guard on the house day and night. He also made Kha his official food taster. He forced her to taste each dish before he would touch it."

"Why?"

"To make sure no one had bribed one of his mistresses to slip him poison," Sen Loi explained.

"Gosh! Wasn't that dangerous for Kha?"

"Yes. She became ill many time, but thanks to her knowledge of herbs, she managed to save herself, each time."

"So, how did your father die?"

"One day Kha got fed up. She had had enough. She couldn't live like that anymore so she made a decision to put an end to it all."

"How?"

"She used the British method."

"The British have a method? A method of doing what?"

"Of poisoning people. Haven't you ever watched a British mystery movie or read a book by the famous writer Agatha Christie?"

"Yes! Arsenic, in the tea!"

"Exactly. One night, while my father was enjoying his late night opium pipe, he called for jasmine tea. And that was when she did it. She made it look as if he died in his sleep."

"Wow! She killed her own son!" Sue Lin said. "That must have been hard for her."

"Oh, indeed it was. She had a nervous breakdown, and even tried to kill herself. But Pug and I managed to keep her alive."

"What about those concubines?"

"Well, they all cried for a while, and then went looking for new men. The members of my father's triad left to join other triads. And I took over my father's interest in the Blue Dragon."

"And you kept the house."

"Of course. And fortunately, my mother had kept and given me, the marriage contract, and my birth certificate, so that made me the sole legal survivor and owner. Later, Kha showed me the secret room behind the bookcase where my father kept all his gold and things of value. I invested it in stocks and bonds, in the bank that Joan's father managed. I also bought a fast race horse, as you know."

"But you are also very generous. You give to charities all the time. You gave Lady St. John a considerable sum for the injured horses. And you send weapons and food north to support the war."

"Oh, no doubt, I am a very charitable person!"

"And sooooo modest!" Sue Lin said. They both laughed.

For a moment they listened as they heard a motorcycle in the distance getting closer and closer, and finally pulling up into the shed outside the house. Five minutes later, Pug was ushered into the great room by a young man dressed in navy tropical whites with matching shoes and hat. He had short, blonde hair, and was very handsome. He wore a belt, holster, and had a pistol stuck against Pug's back.

"Here's the package, mistress."

"Well done, my friend. Did you have any trouble finding him?"

"Not really. The St. John's driver lives in the carriage house, above the Pierce Arrow. He told me the boy was down at the Coast Guard marina, getting ready to go out on pirate patrol. When I mentioned Chung-zi, to him he got very interested. He captured me and I brought him to our lair." Pug burst out laughing.

"What the heck is going on here, madam? Is this some sort of a sick joke? Is Joan in danger or not?" Bobby St. John said in a husky voice. "Why, you're that madam Loi, everyone is talking about, aren't you?"

"What are they saying about me?"

"That the police suspect you of selling Joan into slavery, that's what! I think I'll just take all of you in!"

Sue Lin went up to the young man and leaned against him and kissed him softly on the mouth. Suddenly his hand was empty and she was holding the gun. It happened very quickly.

"I bet Joan never kissed you like that, pretty boy," Sue Lin said, tossing the gun to Pug.

"I say, what's going on here?" Bobby St. John asked.

Sen Loi went to the desk and got Yamaguchi's confession and handed it to Bobby St. John.

"What's this?"

"Just read it, and then you decide," Sen Loi said.

Kha came out of the kitchen with an old, rusty revolver and pointed it at Bobby St. John.

"Hold 'em high, stranger," she said, "or I'll blast you to kingdom come!"

"No, grandmother," Sen Loi said. "Not now."

"Well, if you need help, just holler," Kha said, and went into the kitchen again. Bobby St. John didn't know whether to laugh or not, so he just smiled uncertainly. He finished reading the papers, and handed them back to Sen Loi.

"So you see, Lieutenant, this is your chance to save Joan and get Chung-zi. But you have to do it quickly. Once she's in the hands of the slavers, it's all over for her. Will you go to Shek-Kwu?"

Bobby nodded, looking anxious. "I will, madam."

"Do you have a translator on board your boat?"

"Not at the moment. Why?"

"When you confront Chung-zi, you'll need one. Take my man, Pug."

"Alright."

Pug gave a pained grin. "Who me?"

"Yes, you," Sen Loi said. Then, to the Lieutenant, "Give him a rifle. He's an excellent shot."

"Alright, then, he'll come as my guide, translator, and personal bodyguard. How's that, big fellow?"

Pug shrugged. He was more amused than anything else.

"How many guns do you have on board?" Pug asked as they left.

"Don't worry, we have plenty of firepower. We also have a cannon."

"A cannon, huh? Well, that's nice," Pug said, smiling as he followed the young man out through the kitchen. Moments later the motorcycle was speeding away in the early morning shadows.

Sen Loi went over to her desk and sat down with a big sigh. "I hope fortune smiles on us this day, for Joan's sake."

Kha suddenly appeared, standing in the kitchen door. "Sue Lin, that story Sen Loi told you about her father, my son, was all lies. He was a kind, good, and loving boy. I never killed him."

"Of course you didn't grandmother," Sen Loi said sadly.

"The truth is he was a hardworking, farmer. He got kicked by a mule, and died in the hospital. And that's the truth, so there."

"That is the truth, grandmother," Sen Loi said. She had tears in her eyes.

"Yes, and he was a hero to many. Thousands came to his funeral. Even the Queen of England came."

"That is true, my heart," Sen Loi whispered, trying not to cry.

"And so, Sen Loi, you must apologize to Sue Lin for what you said."

Sen Loi looked at Sue Lin. Her eyes, too, were heavy with tears. "Sue Lin, I apologize for what I said about my father. It was all lies. He was a kind man. Do you forgive me?"

Sue Lin's face was drawn and taut. She was on the verge of crying, also. "Yes, mistress, I forgive you."

Sen Loi stood up and looked at old Kha. "And I apologize to you, to, grandmother. Will you forgive my stupidity?"

Suddenly Kha looked confused. She started into the kitchen, but turned back to say, "Forgive you for what? Have you been a naughty girl today?"

"Yes, I was a naughty girl today. I'm sorry for that, and I love you."

"And I love you, too," Kha sighed and went into the kitchen.

Sue Lin rubbed her eyes. "Wow! Now I'm really confused."

Sen Loi cleared her throat and said, "Well, I guess you'll have to stay confused. And don't ask me any more personal questions."

"Don't worry, I won't." Sue Lin looked over at the kitchen door. "May God's speed be with you, dear Pug!"

"What did you say?"

"I said, 'God speed, dear Pug'."

Sen Loi replied, "British movies, huh?"

"Yes," Sue Lin said.

"In that case, I'll say, Amen."

"That's American."

"Yes," Sen Loi said. She added, under her breath, "Be safe Pug, my friend."

9.

Rays of morning sunlight shone through the windows. Sen Loi lay slumped over her desk with her head cradled in her arms while Sue Lin was in a chair leaning over the table in the great room. She mumbled incoherently. A noise from somewhere outside made the young girl sit up straight and look around. She yawned, stretched, and got up. Shivering, she wrapped her arms around her waist and went over to Sen Loi.

"Wake up, mistress."

Sen Loi sat up and rubbed her eyes. She looked dazed. She checked her watch.

"What time is it?" Sue Lin asked.

"Almost noon. Is Kha up?"

Kha came from the kitchen with a tray of hot tea, toast, and marmalade. Sue Lin followed her to the great room table.

"I'm up. I've been up," Kha said as she set the tray on the table. Sen Loi got up and went and sat across from Sue Lin. They tore into the toast and marmalade as Kha stood watching.

"Did you get any sleep, old one?" Sen Loi asked.

"Oh yes, I slept," Kha said, "and I had another dream."

Sen Loi winked at Sue Lin, as if to say, "Here we go again!"

"What was it, this time?" Sue Lin asked.

"I dreamed a bull attacked a mongoose, and the mongoose turned into a tiger and tore the bull's eyes out and ate its liver," Kha said coldly, without emotion.

"How gruesome!" Sue Lin said. She shivered again.

"And I suppose this strange dream has a meaning, does it not?" Sen Loi asked, as Kha expected her to.

"It means that war is going to come here, big time. The Japanese will kick the British behinds, but the prostitutes of Kowloon will rise up and save the city."

"Oh, is that what it means?"

"Yes."

"And you got all that from a stupid, old dream, grandmother?" Sue Lin chuckled.

Sen Loi frowned at her ward. "I wouldn't mock her if I were you. There's an old saying about not making an enemy of the cook."

"Oh, mock me if you wish, little snail. But mark my words trouble is coming from the north. And the British will end up with their butts swinging in the wind. And I'll say no more about that!" Kha went stomping into the kitchen, muttering under her breath.

"Kha is a bit strange don't you think so, mistress?"

"Why, no. Not at all. She's probably the smartest and sanest person in all of Kowloon."

They sat eating quietly for a moment. Suddenly there were three loud knocks at the door.

"Police! Open up!"

"Poop!" Sue Lin shouted.

"Remind me to wash your mouth out with lye soap," Sen Loi said, quickly getting up from the table.

Before Sen Loi could get to it, the front door swung open and Inspector Marion burst into the foyer.

"You're under arrest, madam! Anything you say will be used against you as evidence at a trial!" the young Inspector said.

"Are you really serious, Inspector?"

"I've never been more serious in my life." Inspector Marion pulled a pair of handcuffs from his jacket pocket and held them up to view. "Need I use these, madam, or will you come peacefully?"

"You're making a terrible mistake, Inspector," Sen Loi said.

"You can tell that to your counselor, madam, and I'd advise you to get one!"

"Do you mind telling me what I'm being charged with?"

The Inspector sneered. "As if you didn't know, madam. Take a wild guess."

"Murder then, is it, Inspector?"

"Exactly! Good guess!"

"The murder of Chief Inspector Barnes, is it?"

"Chief Inspector Barnes? Oh, no. I can't prove that just yet. But I soon will."

"If not Barnes, then who Inspector?"

'I'm taking you in for the murder of Miss Joan Wainwright. But if you want to confess to murdering the Chief Inspector, also, please do. It'll save a lot of time."

Sue Lin, who had been watching from the great room, burst out laughing. It instantly irritated the young Inspector. "I don't see anything funny here, young lady."

"Oh, you will, Inspector, you soon will." Sen Loi said.

"You're wasting my time, madam. Let's go. I'm taking you in."

Suddenly Kha came out of the kitchen carrying the old navy revolver in both hands, trying to hold it steady, pointing it at the police officer.

"One move, you varmint, and I'll blow your head off!"

"Is she serious?" Inspector Marion asked. He wasn't quite sure of what to do. This wasn't in the manual. He froze in place, just to be safe.

"No, she's harmless Inspector," Sen Loi said to the Englishman. And then, to the old woman, "Kha, it's alright. Everything is fine. Isn't that right, Inspector?"

"Ah, yes, everything is just fine."

"So you say!" Kha stayed in place. The gun wobbled in her tiny hands. It was so heavy it took all her strength to hold it straight.

Sue Lin went over to the desk and picked up Yamaguchi's confession. "Why don't you show him this confession, mistress?"

"Oh, so you wrote out a confession did you?" Inspector Marion said. "Well, that will do it for you, madam." He motioned to Sue Lin. "Hand it over, if you please."

Sue Lin handed the sheet of papers to the Inspector who jammed them carelessly into a jacket pocket without looking at it.

"Alright, it's time to go madam."

"Maybe you should read the confession first, Inspector?" Sue Lin said, smiling seductively.

Inspector Marion glanced nervously over at Kha and the revolver. "No hurry. I'll read it soon enough."

Kha exploded. "Read it now, you white worm! Read it!"

The Inspector flinched as if smacked in the face. He quickly took the papers out of his pocket. The women watched and waited as he began reading.

Finally the Inspector cleared his throat. "Where did you get this?" He waved the confession in the air.

"Does it matter?"

"How do I know it's authentic? Or if it wasn't gotten by torture?"

"Oh, it's authentic, alright, Inspector," Sue Lin said, "and there's more."

Sue Lin picked up the intelligence report and gave it to the police officer. "How about this?"

"What, another confession? We're full of confession this morning, aren't we?"

The Inspector glanced nervously at Kha and her gun again, then held the report up and began reading it.

"As you can see, the barber was also a spy," Sen Loi said. "I'm sure Naval Intelligence would like to question him, wouldn't you say so, Inspector?"

"Again, Madam, where did you get this?"

"Does it matter?"

"How do I know these papers are authentic? Or that they were gotten by legal means?"

"Forget about what is legal and what's not legal," Sen Loi said. "Think in terms of bringing a spy to justice, of national defense, and saving British lives. Wouldn't you like to be the man who broke up a spy ring? You'd be a national hero, Inspector. Wouldn't that mean a promotion? Perhaps to Chief Inspector?"

For a moment the young man was at a loss for words. He shifted uncertainly on his feet, planning out his next move.

Sen Loi continued. "Look, Inspector. I'm not going anywhere. I have deep roots here in Kowloon, as you well know. Why not go and check the barber out. If I'm wrong, then come back and arrest me. I'll be right here."

Marion cleared his throat. He glanced at Kha. "Could you please tell the old one to stop pointing that thing at me? I'm afraid it might accidently discharge."

Sen Loi turned to Kha. "It's alright, Kha. You can go now."

Kha wiped her nose with the back of one hand, as she had seen it done in American westerns.

"Are you sure? I could drop this skunk like a lead nickel!" Kha said in her best cowboy voice.

"No, everything is fine," Sen Loi, insisted. Kha nodded, sniffed, and disappeared back into the kitchen.

"You'll have to forgive her," Sen Loi said. "She been going to those horrible American cowboy movies. And the pistol isn't loaded."

"Well, perhaps you should do something about her?"

"About the barber? Do we have a deal?"

"Not until I confirm the authenticity of these papers," the Inspector said. "And, I'm taking you in until I do."

"That would be a foolish move, Inspector," Sen Loi said.

"Is that a threat? It sounds like one, Madam!"

"No, no, Inspector. I'm only suggesting that if you arrest me, you could end up, as you British say, with egg on your face. Or looking very foolish, at the least."

"Oh? And why is that?"

"Because there are some things happening at this very moment that, if you arrest me, can make you look very, well, stupid."

The Inspector was quiet for a moment, then he said, "Really, now. What things are you referring to?"

"Even as we speak, Lieutenant Robert St. John of the British Coast Guard is on his way to Shek Kwu Island to save Joan Wainwright from the pirate Chung-zi."

The Inspector chuckled. "Who told you that fairytale, Madam?"

"It's no fairytale, sir. In fact, my man, Pug, has gone along to assist them."

"Your driver, Pug? What a ridiculous story!" Marion said contemptuously.

"I'm very serious, Inspector?" Sen Loi said. "If you arrest me, I'll sue you. And I must warn you, I have the best lawyers in all of Kowloon. They have never lost a case. When they are finished with you, sir, you will be the laughing stock of Kowloon, and be reduced in rank to Assistant Detective. Do you want to chance that?"

For a moment the Inspector was stunned by the attack.

"You're bluffing?" he said uncertainly.

"If you believe that, then go ahead and arrest me Inspector."

The Inspector looked at the papers again. He studied them more closely. Finally he folded them neatly and put them in the breast pocket of his coat. He let out a big sigh of resignation.

"Do you swear to me that you're telling the truth?"

"Yes."

"On your family's honor?"

"If I must, then yes, on my family's honor."

"Alright, then," the Inspector said grudgingly. "But you are still on house arrest. You understand that, don't you?"

"Of, course," Sen Loi said. "But there's one more thing."

"What's that?"

"My car. It's still missing."

"Oh, yes. Alright, I'll see what I can do."

"Thank you, Inspector."

There was nothing more to be said. The Inspector went to the door. He stood with his back to the others.

"I'm not a bad person, you know. I'm just trying to do my job. It's not easy."

Inspector Marion went out and in a short while drove away.

Sue Lin chuckled. "I think he likes you, Mistress."

"No one asked you."

"Yeah, I saw how he looks at you," Sue Lin said, laughing.

"Oh, be quiet you stupid girl."

Kha came from the kitchen, wiping her hands on a towel. "What's so funny?"

"Nothing," Sue Lin said.

"Only fools laugh at nothing," Kha said.

"Do you think he'll arrest the barber, Mistress?" Sue Lin asked.

"I doubt it. Yamaguchi has probably left the country by now, rather than chance being hung by the British."

"The young Inspector could turn out to be a big hero, Mistress. And all because of you."

"Well," Kha said, "don't expect any gratitude. That dim-witted limey couldn't track down a six-legged elephant without our help."

Sen Loi and Sue Lin burst out laughing.

"That's it, old one, no more going to see American movies for you!"

10.

It was mid-afternoon, a week later. Sue Lin was sitting at the dining table reading the newspaper while Sen Loi was at her desk doing paperwork. Pug sat in a chair next to her, his right arm in a sling. He had a large, blue ribbon with a gold pendant around his neck, and was wearing a new chauffeur's uniform. He fingered the pendant, looking over at Sue Lin.

"Aw, come on, read it one more time!" he called over to her.

"Nope! Three times was enough!"

"Aw, come on little flower, please?"

"Alright, but this is absolutely the last time. Do you hear me?"

"I hear you. The last time. Absolutely."

"Alright, the last time." Sue Lin cleared her throat and read, "'In a daring predawn raid under the command of Coast Guard Naval Officer, Lieutenant Robert St. John, Jr., the son of noted Hong Kong socialite, and widow, Lady Jane St. John, the human slave trade in the South China Sea was dealt a severe blow…'"

"The little twerp did pretty well," Pug cut in, chuckling.

"Don't interrupt!" Sue Lin said.

"Oh, sorry." Pug said.

Sue Lin continued where she had left off. "Let me see…'During the ferocious battle between the Naval Marines and the pirates, nine slavers were killed and ten were taken prisoner. Among those captured was the notorious pirate known as Chung-zi, who has been on the government's most wanted list for over nine years.'"

As Sue Lin paused to turn the page, Pug said, "Here comes the good part."

"Of course," Sen Loi chuckled.

Sue Lin resumed reading: "Here it is…' Assisting the British forces was one Shashi-Benshu, known as 'Pug' Benshu.'" At this point Sue Lin burst out laughing. When she finally stopped, she said, "Sorry, Shashi!" Once the word was out of her mouth she had another fit of laughter. After that was over, she wiped the tears from her eyes.

"That stupid reporter said he wouldn't use my whole name. Wait until I see him," Pug growled.

Sue Lin read on, "'Mr. Benshu, who went along as a guide, was wounded as he shielded the kidnapped British socialite, Miss Joan Wainwright, by throwing himself into the line of fire, thereby saving her life.'"

Sen Loi smiled at Pug. "Why don't you tell Sue Lin what really happened, Pug?"

"I didn't throw myself into the line of fire, little one."

"You didn't?"

"No."

"But it says here…"

"I know, but the truth is, Joan jumped behind me just as the pirate shot at her. I took a bullet in the arm that was meant for her."

"That's awful," Sue Lin said.

"Well, I got a medal out of it, and I'm now very well liked by those British snobs over in Hong Kong!"

Sue Lin turned a newspaper page and scanned the headlines. "Oh, look! Here's an article about Inspector Marion!"

"What does it say?" Pug asked.

"I'll read it," Sue Lin said. "Let's see…'Acting on a tip from a confidential source, Police Inspector John Marion uncovered a foreign spy ring ran by a local barber here in Kowloon. Certain incriminating documents were found in the possession of Jin-su Yamaguchi. These documents revealed that he was sending intelligence reports about British naval vessels, their routes, armaments, and the number of British troops stationed here in Kowloon and Hong Kong, to foreign sources. Mr. Yamaguchi was apprehended at the airport in Hong Kong just as he was about to fly to Singapore. As a result of his work and dedication to his country, Inspector Marion is being promoted to Chief Inspector.'"

"Well, how about that?" Pug said. "And he owes it all to you, Mistress."

"To us, Pug…to all of us."

Sue Lin pouted. "We do the work, he gets the glory, and we get nothing."

Sen Loi smiled. "Perhaps…perhaps not. But I think he will be needing us now, more than ever."

"Oh, how so, Mistress?" Pug asked.

"We're the best source of information that he has. Our underground informant network is the best in Kowloon. And I'm sure he knows it. If not, he soon will," Sen Loi said. "I suspect we'll be seeing a lot of Inspector Marion in the coming days."

Pug chuckled. "So, we sort of own him. Do we mistress?"

"Sort of? I'd say, positively." Sen Loi said

Sue Lin's face lit up. "Oh, look! Here's a piece about Joan! It says…'Lady St. John announces the upcoming marriage of her son, Lieutenant Robert St. John to the British banking heiress and socialite, Miss Joan Wainwright of Kowloon, in June.' Good for Joan! At last she can be happy!"

"That remains to be seen," Sen Loi said.

"I wonder what happened to her rotten uncle?" Pug asked. "He seems to have disappeared from the face of the earth."

"I think Lady St. John and her people put an end to him. Packed him off to jolly, old England. They can't afford a scandal in the family," Sen Loi said. "These Brits are sensitive about such matters."

Sue Lin asked, "I wonder if Joan knew how he betrayed her?"

"Probably not. And maybe it's best that way," Sen Loi said.

"I wonder if she will come to visit us again?" Sue Lin mused.

"I'm sure Joan's calendar will be full for a long while," Sen Loi said. "What with social teas and gatherings, and getting married, she'll barely have any time for herself, I would think."

"I really like her, Mistress. I'll miss her a lot," Sue Lin said sadly.

"We all will, won't we Pug?" Sen Loi said.

Before Pug could answer, a car pulled up in the courtyard. Someone knocked. Sue Lin put down the paper. Pug and Sen Loi watched as the young girl went and opened the door.

"Joan!" Sue Lin said eagerly. "We were just talking about you!"

Joan Wainwright laughed as she walked into the foyer. She gave Sue Lin a warm hug, then went to Sen Loi, and shook her hand.

"Oh, Madam Loi, how I have missed you!" the British girl said, excitedly. She turned to Pug. "Pug, my hero! My dearest friend! How are you?"

Pug blushed. "I'm fine. Thank you for asking, Miss Wainwright."

Joan turned back to Sen Loi again. "Madam Loi, how good to see you again."

"We were just about to take tea, Joan. Won't you join us?"

"For a little while, yes. I just happened to be in the area. I'm to meet Bobby later at the marina."

"I'll go rustle up some grub," Sue Lin said and hurried off into the kitchen.

Joan chuckled. "She's been going to the cinema, to those American westerns, hasn't she?"

"Yes, her, Pug, and Kha have been sneaking off. I'll have to stop that."

Sen Loi took Joan's arm and led her into the great room and Pug went into the kitchen. The two women sat across from each other at the table. Joan suddenly looked troubled. She stared down at her handbag.

"Are you alright, Joan? You seem..."

The girl looked up and forced a smile. "Oh, no, I'm fine, really fine."

Sen Loi studied the girl's face. She looked older and worn. That vibrant innocence she had shown before was now gone. Behind that forced façade of happiness Sen Loi could see fear and terror.

"It was that ordeal that you recently went through, Joan, isn't it? Do you want to talk about it?"

Joan looked away, then back. "What! Oh, the kidnapping? No, I've gotten over that."

"No, Joan, you haven't. Not yet. It'll take a long time before the scars heal. You're having horrible dreams now, aren't you?"

Joan suddenly broke down and sobbed, covering her face in her hands to hide her embarrassment. The older woman reached across the table and put a hand on her arm.

"It was horrible!" Joan blurted out.

"I know they did unspeakable things to you Joan, but you must forgive them. Let the hate go, Joan. They were not human…they were animals. They were against all that is humane and decent. That is why Bobby hunted them down and killed them. They were not fit to live."

"Yes, I know I should let it go, but I just can't, not yet! And, over there, they don't understand! They don't even try to understand!"

"Oh?"

"In Hong Kong it's all, 'stiff upper lip,' and, 'carry on old girl.' I can't make them see it…they won't even listen! They expect me to, 'suck it up,' and 'march on.' Everything will be, 'hunky dory.' It's like nothing ever happened to me. I can't talk to them!" The girl's body shook from sobbing.

"I see," Sen Loi said.

Suddenly Joan stopped crying. She looked up. "Is my eye makeup running?"

"No, you look beautiful, as always," Sen Loi said. "Ah, how are you and Lady St. John getting on? Well, I hope?"

Joan paused to think whether to say it or not, then did. "We don't see eye-to-eye at all. She's become very authoritative and very dominating."

Sen Loi smiled. "But that's only natural, Joan. It's called a 'pecking order.' You'll be in the St. John clan soon, you see."

"Yes, and they outnumber me. It's as if she's my mother as well as Bobby's. And with him, it's, 'Mother said this,' or 'Mother said that,' or 'Mother doesn't permit this,' or 'Mother doesn't permit that.' I'm really getting fed up with it!"

"You're not having second thoughts about your marriage, are you, Joan?"

"Oh, I don't know. I just don't know."

Sen Loi got up and sat in a chair alongside Joan. She put an arm around the girl's shoulder.

"Look, Joan," the older woman said, "You've been through a horrible ordeal, and now, on top of that, you have to adjust to a new reality." She held back a moment then said, "Do you want my advice?"

"Oh, yes! Please!"

"Do you love Bobby?"

"Oh, yes, I do!"

"Then fight for him. You survived those dreadful pirates, so surely you can survive Lady St. John. You are younger and stronger than her. Every day she will grow weaker and you will grow stronger. With each child you give Bobby, the more he will love you, and the stronger your position will be. And all the more Lady St. John will have to respect you. Do you understand what I'm saying, Joan?"

"Yes, I think so." The girl was smiling now. She had hung onto every word, and each word had opened her eyes and cleared her mind, and made her feel more secure and stronger.

"Because of your ordeal, the bonds between you and Bobby are deeper than ever. She can never take that from you two." Pausing to let the words sink in. "Joan, your life is just beginning. Live it. Live it as hard and as full as you can.

Go to Bobby and tell him how much you love and need him."

Joan's face lit up with the realization of the power she could have.

"I shall! I shall! Oh, Madam Loi, thank you so much!" They both stood up. Joan adjusted her hair and dress.

"And remember, Joan, I will always be here if you should need my help."

The girl threw her arms around Sen Loi for a moment, then backed away, embarrassed.

"I'm sorry."

"No. I like a good hug now and then," Sen Loi said, laughing.

She led Joan to the door. The girl left, and the sound of her car soon faded away. Sue Lin came out of the kitchen with the tea tray. She looked around.

"Where's Joan?"

"Something came up and she had to leave."

"It must have been important," Sue Lin said. She put the tray on the dining table.

"Yes, it was."

"She comes and goes, just like that?"

"Yes."

"Did you say something to her?"

"We talked."

"Well, she came here looking happy and all of a sudden she leaves. Did you say something to hurt her?"

"Believe me, she is just fine. Now let's have tea."

Sen Loi sat down. "Where's Pug?"

"Why? Do you need him?"

"No, I only wondered where he is. That's all."

"He's out in the garage, working on the motor cycle.

"That's all I wanted to know."

"Well, now you know." Sue Lin said bluntly, sitting down with a sour look on her face.

"Look, I know you're upset because Joan left, but she'll be back."

"When?"

"Soon. She said soon."

"Probably never!"

"Look, Sue Lin, I wouldn't become too attached to Joan, if I were you. She lives in a different world than we do."

"I'm not attached to her. She's nice and I like her, that's all."

"Well, you should be careful. You might get hurt."

"How would I get hurt? We like each other, that's all. And we're friends."

Sen Loi stared at her young ward and shook her head. "No. Joan isn't your friend, Sue Lin. Listen to me, if you ever chance to run into Joan at the racetrack or somewhere on the street in town, and she's with her people, don't expect her to stop and talk to you. In fact she just might pretend not to know you at all."

Sue Lin's eyes narrowed. "I don't think she would do that! Why do you say such a thing, Mistress?"

"Tell me, what do you really think we are to Joan?"

"Like I said, we're friends!"

Sen Loi looked away for a moment, searching for the right words. She finally stared back at the young girl and said, "What we are to Joan is a place to hide. When the pressure is too much for her in her world, she will come here and unload her cares and problems and then go away feeling better. When she needs sympathy and understanding, and can't get it in her world, she'll come here to get it. But she doesn't want us taking part in her world."

Sue Lin glared across the table at her Mistress. "You did that to her, you made her like that. Didn't you?"

"It's what she wanted. From the first day she came here, I sensed it. So I gave it to her."

"And now she worships you! She'll do anything you tell her to do or believe anything you say, won't she."

"Oh, don't worry. One day she'll wake up and she'll realize that everybody in Kowloon uses everybody. For good or bad, we use each other. So don't get all choked up about poor Joan."

"So, some day she'll be just like us? She'll lose that sweetness and honesty that makes her Joan?"

"And the sooner she does the better chance she'll have to survive the St. Johns."

Sue Lin shrunk in on herself and sighed. "Well, I like her just the way she is."

"As do I, but she needs to change to survive in Hong Kong," Sen Loi said softly, trying to make Sue Lin understand. "They play rough in Lady St' John's circle. They are cynical and cruel, and they will walk all over Joan. She's got to adapt and quickly. And I'm going to help her."

"You mean, control her, don't you?"

Suddenly they heard the sound of a car engine coming up the driveway, into the courtyard. In a few moments someone was knocking at the front door again.

"We're having a busy morning," Sen Loi said.

"It might be Joan!" Sue Lin jumped up and ran to the door and flung it open. Chief Inspector Marion nodded and stepped into the foyer. Sen Loi went to meet him. They stood face to face.

"Chief Inspector Marion…what a pleasant surprise, sir." She waved a hand at Sue Lin. The girl went quickly into the kitchen.

Marion bowed politely. "Madam Loi."

"Is this an official or a social call, Chief Inspector?"

"Both, madam."

"Both, is it? Well, then, which would you like to start with, Chief Inspector?"

"First off, I'd like to apologize for my, ah, previous…"

"Your aggressive nature?"

"That and my rudeness and unprofessional conduct," Marion said. "Chief Inspector Barnes's papers revealed how you helped him with several difficult cases."

"I did what little I could. Chief Inspector Barnes and I were good friends."

"Well, I'm grateful for your help during recent events…the Yamaguchi and Wainwright cases. I won't forget how helpful you were."

"There's no need to thank me, Chief Inspector," Sen Loi said. Marion looked around the foyer for a moment, saying nothing more, as if he was feeling a bit awkward. "Is there something else, Chief Inspector?"

"Ah…actually, yes." The Englishman reached into his coat pocket and took out a small, rectangular, cloth-covered, blue box. He handed it to Sen Loi.

"A present, for me?"

"Just a small token of Her Majesty's gratitude, madam."

Sen Loi opened the box and stared at its contents.

"What? A medal for me?"

"It's called the, 'Exceptional Service in Defense of the British Nation,' award."

"I'm overwhelmed."

"They don't give out many of those to…"

"I'm sure they don't," Sen Loi cut in. "And that makes it all the more precious."

The Chief Inspector reached into his inside coat breast pocket and took out a large, brown envelope and gave it to Sen Loi. "And this is an official letter of notification that goes with the medal. Explaining the details of why it was given."

"How nice."

"It's the least we could do, Madam." Marion said. He seemed at a loss for more words.

"Is there anything else, Chief Inspector?"

"No. We just wanted you to know that we appreciate what you did." A silence followed those last words. There was nothing more to be said. "Well, then, Madam, I must be getting on. Things to do, you know. Loose ends to tie up. That sort of thing."

"Yes, that sort of thing."

"No rest for the weary, you know."

"How true."

"Well, good-day to you, then."

"And a very good-day to you, too, Chief Inspector."

Chief Inspector Marion started towards the front door.

"Chief Inspector!" Sen Loi said.

Marion turned to face Sen Loi.

"Madam?"

"Do you play chess, sir?"

"Actually, I do, but only at a layman's level, I'm afraid."

"Chief Inspector Barnes would come Sunday evenings. But he wasn't married, of course."

"Oh, really?"

"Yes, we would have wine and smoke a cigar. We would do more talking than playing."

Marion chuckled. "I can't see you smoking a cigar, Madam."

"Oh, but I sometimes do, on certain occasions."

"And I bet he brought flowers and a box of sweets."

"Yes, he did. The old flirt. And sometimes he would bring me the latest mystery by Agatha Christie."

"What a coincidence. She's one of my favorites. Do you have her latest?"

"Unfortunately, I don't."

"Well, it so happens that I do. It's absolutely ripping!"

"Oh, now, that sounds intriguing! I shall have to get a copy!"

"Nonsense! I'll lend you my copy, if you want."

"Are you sure?"

"Absolutely! I'll bring it next Sunday, if that's alright."

"Yes. Sunday would be fine."

"Evening?"

"Yes, about six?"

"Alright, then, six it is." The Chief Inspector nodded and turned and left. Moments later Pug, Kha, and Sue Lin came into the foyer to join their mistress.

"I suppose you three had your ears to the door, no doubt," Sen Loi said.

"Oh, yes," Pug said. "We didn't miss a word. The sap is in love with you."

"I wonder if he's married?" Sue Lin asked.

"No, he isn't married," Sen Loi said.

"How do you know that, Mistress?" Sue Lin replied.

"Two things. He doesn't smell married and he doesn't wear a wedding ring."

They all laughed.

"He's no Chief Inspector Barnes, that's for sure," Pug said.

"Not yet," Sen Loi said, "but I think someday he will be."

"I'm sure you'll see to that, mistress," Sue Lin chuckled.

"You better not get too palsy-walsy with that gringo," Kha sneered. "He looks like trouble, to me!"

Sen Loi hugged the old woman as Sue Lin and Pug burst into a volley of laughter that took a long time to end. "No more American movies for you, my love!"

THE END

About the Author

R. Annan is a seasoned and traveled author with many interests. As a career serviceman he served in Korea and Vietnam. He also completed a one-year course at the Defense Language Institute at Monterey, California, and graduated from the University of South Florida with a B.A. in Art and Art History. After taking a two-year course in screenwriting at the Hollywood Scriptwriting Institute, he established *The Old Time Radio Club Time Machine* as both a scriptwriter and an actor.

He currently has many short novels in the works: *Mr. Dobbs: A Christmas Ghost Story*; *The Ghost of Reginald Burton, Esquire; Vzor's Prisoner: A Sci-fi Novel; The Princess of Ovaar: A Sci-fi Fantasy; The Barnhart Intruder; Elke: A Love Story; The Fight for the Lazy M: A Western;* and *The Gunfighter in Winter: A Jack Cordell Western*. Look for these and other books to appear soon.

A Note from the Author

If you've enjoyed this book, would you please consider rating it and reviewing it? Here's a link to find all my books on Amazon www.amazon.com/author/rannan Thank you!

www.ingramcontent.com/pod-product-compliance
Lightning Source LLC
Chambersburg PA
CBHW060617130626
46555CB00002B/540